ALL IN ONE

All In One

A Collection Of Short Stories

Mable Inetta Cox

Mable I. Cox
Fort Washington, MD

The author has chosen to capitalize specific words relating to the Lord and His Kingdom and any pronouns preferring to the Deity. The author also has chosen to not capitalize respectfully the name of satan or any names relating to his kingdom; e.g., devil and (the) enemy.

Cover design by TLH Designs, Chicago, IL, www.tlhdesigns.com
Book design by Kingdom Living Publishing, Accokeek, MD
www.kingdomlivingbooks.com

For information about this book or to contact the author, write to:

Mable I. Cox
P.O. Box 441035
Fort Washington, Maryland 20744

You may also connect with the author via her website:
www.mablecox.com

Published by:

Mable I. Cox
Fort Washington, MD

Printed in the United States of America.

ISBN 978-0-578-54338-3
ISBN 978-0-578-54339-0 (Ebook)

Dedication

I dedicate this book to my sisters and brother: Ruth Marie Cox, Amelia Hill, Barbara Jones, and Milton Cox, Jr. Thank you for your encouragement and love. God Bless You. Be inspired to use the gift God placed in you and always remember the gift God gave us, our parents Milton and Ruth Cox.

Be blessed and go forward in the gift that the Lord your God has given you.

Contents

He Stopped The Pain

For twenty years or more I had been in pain. It had been a constant nagging pain that seemed to have started in the center of my heart and settled in the bottom of my stomach. It made me nauseated, but most of the time it was a sick feeling that was unexplainable. It was external and internal pain. The pain affected me mentally, physically, and emotionally. It dried up the tears that wanted to fall; it caused scars inside and outside of my body and opened wounds that festered all the time. The smell of pus and sores caused an unbearable odor that made others sick when they were near me. It was a walking ulcer and help was impossible to find. This pain kept me unhealthy and unbalanced in every area of my life. It caused disappointments, let downs, frustration, and depression; and I cursed the day of its inception. It caused hate and anger. It caused me to want to kill and hurt those who truly loved me. It caused me to disrespect my Creator. This pain that I carried around like an albatross hanging around my neck allowed me to do things that made me ashamed. It caused me to be afraid to believe. It caused me to have low self-esteem and even dislike myself. This pain, oh how I tried desperately to stop this pain; it was devastating, and then one day I heard someone talk about Him. I listened attentively and then one day I met Him. He Counselor was considerate and nice. He understood me. We talked about my past experiences. He told me that my past experiences had caused me to disrespect others. He was so honest, loving, and easy to talk with; He solved my problems. He gave me strength, joy, peace, and a reason to live. He accepted me as the person I was. He healed my wounds. He comforted me; He consoled me; He walked and talked with me. He protected me from all dangers. He gave me all that He had. He gave me light so that darkness would never enter my life. He adored me; He removed the anger, frustration, and hate that was in my life. He gave me the power to love myself and others. He taught me things that I never knew, and He took me places that I had never gone. He promised never to leave me, but be with me forever. He gave me His name to use in times of trouble. He introduced me to His Father, and His Father placed His Spirit inside of me; He gave me a language that I could use to speak directly to Him; He made me a part of His family. He called me His child.

He wants to help you. He wants you to become a part of Him. He wants to protect you from the evils of this world. He wants to love you and care for you. He wants to be there in your good and bad times. He wants to be with you forever. He is everything to me, and He wants to be everything to you. He wants to introduce Himself to you.

His name is JESUS, and His name is above all names.

Joy Comes In The Morning

Death knocked at my door many times, and I pulled through, but this time, it was just a matter of one week and I would be faced with my Creator (The Most High God, the One who sent His son Jesus Christ to die so that I would live eternally). I was not afraid of dying; it was something that I knew would happen. At 85 years of age, I had lived a good life. At age 25, I accepted Jesus in my life. My life had many setbacks, trials, tribulations, heartaches, and pains, but I held on to "God's unchanging hand." I had held on to God concerning this illness, but to be just plain old selfish, I was ready to go to my heavenly home; I was ready to die. I had prepared everyone, and everyone had accepted me leaving and was dealing with it in their own way. My husband, Tom, died five years ago. He left me when he was 80 years old. He was ready to die, too. I knew it, and I was at peace with his decision.

Rodell, my oldest son, was taking my wanting to leave this earth very hard. Out of my five children, he was the only one who was not married and did not have any children. He kept telling me not to leave him. He said that he wanted me to stay around long enough to see him married. We both laughed when I would say, "How long, when will that be when I get 110? Rodell was my favorite. Most parents say that they don't have a favorite, but I think most mothers do. You know, it is something about that first child. It is not that you do not love the others, but that first one brings experiences that are hard to compare to the others. Rodell really loved me I could tell. The other children were there, but their families took some of their time. Rodell was always around. I could count on him to call every day, come by weekends, and introduce me to any new girl in his life. To be very honest, I don't think Rodell wanted to get married. I really felt he liked the single life. He had nice lady friends. Almost all of them were sweet and nice. I would not have minded having any of them for a daughter-in-law. He did act as if he was very interested in one, but he just laughed when I would ask, "When are you going to marry her?"

Lori, my second oldest, was married and had two children. She looked just like her father. She was two years younger than Rodell, but he always felt he had to take care of his sister. I remembered when Lori was preparing for her wedding. Before I could give her the final mother to daughter talk, Rodell did. He read every book he could find related to marriage and relationships and talked to her about what she should and should not do. Lori was very proud of her brother. Like a good sister, she listened to every word he said. She never told him to use that advice for himself. She just listened as he talked and talked.

Donna and Donnell were the twins in the family. I did not know I was having twins until the day I was in the delivery room. Two at one time! I did not know what to say or do when the doctor said there was another one. They were seven years younger than Rodell. I think Rodell and Lori thought they were dolls. Donna and Donnell were the talk of the family discussions at dinner time. Everyone wanted to know what interesting task they performed during the day. They wanted to know if they cried or smiled at the same time. Donna and Donnell were always close. Not only were they twins, but they were also best friends. They had a double wedding, and both of them have three children.

Sophia was born two years after the twins. It was almost impossible to believe that I was pregnant again. I had two-year-old twins and a baby. Sophia grew up to be a lovely young lady. She married at eighteen and had five children. I guess she was determined to follow in my footsteps. She was a quiet child and a loner. When she told me that she and her high school sweetheart were planning on getting married, I just looked at her. She said, "I know you think I am too young, but we will be okay."

Tom was always there for the children and me. He was very supportive and loving. When he felt I needed a break, he would put all the children in the van and take them for a ride. He was a good father. I guess I can say I knew that when I first met him.

I met Tom Jenkins at church. I was sitting beside my mother, listening to Rev. McCarthy when I turned to my left and caught his eye. He looked at me, I looked at him, and we both smiled at each other. It was love at first sight for him.

Tom was the oldest of ten children. I would see him every Sunday sitting beside his father, Mr. Tom Jenkins, Sr. I had never paid any attention to him until that day. He would always walk in the church with his father and the other nine would come in with his mother. We worshipped at a small church, so everyone would turn around when they walked in. They were like little ducklings following the mother duck. I should not have been shocked when I had twins because his mother and father had three sets. It was shocking. Everyone talked about her. The older people said someone put a curse on her. They also said that they thought Tom was a twin too; maybe the other one died. They were the talk of the church almost every Sunday. All of the children were clean and neatly dressed. The girls' hair was always pretty with ribbons or barrettes on almost every braid.

Mrs. Sara, Tom's mother, made her clothes and her children's clothes, and she did an outstanding job. Mrs. Sarah could do almost anything. She was a great cook. When the church had family day, everyone would stand around her basket to get a piece of her coconut pineapple cake and her fried chicken. Mrs. Sarah's chicken and cake were the highlights of the event.

Tom loved his mother. He did everything he could to make it easy on her. It was not unusual to see him get up during church service and take the baby from his mother. Everyone admired Tom Jr. for being such a gentleman, and the day I looked at him, he was holding the baby. He held the baby with his strong hands, and anytime the baby would cry, he would rock the baby so gently. I looked at him and he looked at me, and we both smiled.

After service, he gave his mother the baby and walked right in my direction. I just sat there knowing he was coming to talk to me. Tom walked right in front of me and said hello. I said hello back. He asked how I enjoyed the service, and I told him it was fine. He then asked me if I could date. I looked at him and smiled. I asked him if he was asking if he could come by the house and see me. He smiled and said he would love that. He said that he wanted to get to know me better. I smiled; and then he said that he would ask my father if it was okay. Before I could say anything, Tom left and almost ran to my father. He was a bold young man. He was standing right in front of my father talking. All of a sudden, I saw Tom and my father walking in my direction. I did not know what to expect. My father walked over to me and said that he had known Tom's father for years. He said that he was a good man and he knew when Tom was born. He said Tom was a good boy and if my mother and his parents did not have any problems, Tom would be welcomed at his house. Tom ran to my mother and gave her the information before my father could tell her. I saw my mother smiling and nodding her head. Tom ran back and said it was okay. I asked him what his parents said. He told me that he had talked to them about me already. He said they were just waiting for him to say something to my parents and me. Tom was smiling and told me that he would see me later that afternoon.

Tom was coming to the house. I did not know how to feel. He arrived a minute earlier than his expected time. I could not believe that he was there. Dinner was on the table, so my father asked him to have dinner with us. Tom said yes before my father could tell him what was for dinner. He asked where he could wash his hands and where they wanted him to sit at the table.

Dinner was the best. Mom had cooked some fried chicken and collards, and she had made potato salad, hot buttered rolls, and an apple pie for dessert. Tom enjoyed himself. I immediately got up from the table and began washing the dishes. My sisters and brother scattered. I guess they felt it was not a good time for them to be around. Mom helped me dry the dishes while Tom and my father sat in the living room and talked.

After washing the dishes, I walked into the living room to talk to Tom. My father got up quickly as if someone was calling him. He told Tom he would talk to him later. Tom said okay and stared at me. He was dressed nicely. He had changed from the suit he had on at church. He had on a pair of blue pants, white shirt, blue shoes, and a blue tie. Tom was a neat dresser. He always looked nice in his clothes. Some of his clothes were purchased, but most of his clothes came from Roger Allen. His father worked for Mr. Bob Allen and when his son Roger outgrew his clothes, they went to Tom. Mr. Bob was a nice man. He seemed to like Tom's family. I would hear my mom and some of the neighbors talk about all of the things that Mr. Bob Allen had given Tom's family. Mr. Bob paid Tom's father decent money and even helped him purchase their house. At one time, they used to live on Mr. Bob's property, but Mr. Bob wanted them to have their own space. He told Mr. Tom Sr. that he should have property to leave his children when he and his wife passed away. Mr. Tom respected Mr. Bob. He listened and took a lot of his advice. With the children that Mr. Tom and Mrs. Sara had, they were not financially able to do a lot of things. Tom's dad was a good man. He took good care of his family, and he was always helping people in need. He would help people paint their houses, paint the church, work on cars, etc. He was always fixing up the church. The older people used to tease him and say he was there more than the preacher. They would also say he should have been the one preaching since he was there most of the time. Mr. Tom would just smile and keep doing whatever task he was trying to complete.

Tom Jr. acted as if he was really enjoying himself. We talked about everything. He was sweating a lot. I guess he was nervous. I was fine. It was as if I had known him all of my life. He kept wiping his face with his handkerchief, so I asked him if he wanted some iced tea. He thanked me, and I went into the kitchen to get him a glass. While there, I decided to bring him a piece of pound cake that I had baked the night before. I was not sure where this visit would go, so I decided to let him taste some of my cooking. When I went back outside, he was gone; but I heard voices. He was in my father's garden talking to him. I guess he felt that if he could impress my father, then he would have my heart. I just looked at him and smiled. I called him, and he ran to me. He apologized for not being where I left him. I just looked at him. He took the tea and the cake. Before I sat down, half of the cake was gone. He asked who baked it. I told him I did. He complimented me on the cake and told me that it was the best pound cake he had ever tasted. He looked at me and said that if we got married, at least you can cook. I looked at him and asked him what that meant. He told me that he had been noticing me for some time. He said he would watch me almost every Sunday. He said he watched me when I walked into the church and when I left church. He said that he had even asked my sisters and brothers about me. I just stared at him. He said that he never took his eyes off me. He said he just did not know how to approach me, but he finally got up enough nerves, and he was glad he did. He said that today was a good day, and it was great that Ernest was not at church. I asked him why he mentioned Ernest. He said because during the time he was watching me, I was watching Ernest. I laughed and said after last week and all the things that happened, my watching Ernest was over. Tom laughed too.

Ernest was the preacher's son. He was light skinned with green eyes. All the girls liked him, and he liked all the girls. He was about two years older than I was. We sang in the choir together and every fifth Sunday we ushered together.

Ernest was so articulate and smart. He knew what to say and how to say it. His words would melt a girl's heart. He was so smooth talking and sweet. I guess that was what he did to Millie. He melted her heart so much that he got her pregnant. Last Sunday they got married. Yes, it was almost a "shotgun wedding" because Millie's father told the preacher that if his boy did not marry his daughter and give the baby his name that he would kill him. This was the conversation some of the old women had when they would see each other. Mr. Boone, Millie's father, meant every word he said, and everybody knew that he did. Mr. Boone was nice in his own way. He was very outspoken and did not "bite his tongue" when he talked about his gun and killing people; everyone listened. He had been in jail when he was younger. He did not mind telling anyone that he had been, and if someone bothered him, he would go again. He was always talking about all the animals he killed and how he killed them. He was one of the deacons in the church. When he spoke, all of the other deacons listened. I wondered if he was a deacon because they were too afraid not to give him a position in the church.

Ernest was so attractive. He was the first guy that I knew that was promised an academic scholarship to the local Christian college. He was smart. He could tell you about any story, play, or poem, and he knew a little Shakespeare. He also was able to speak some French. His French teacher was a member of the church. She would always speak French to him when she saw him on Sundays. He loved math too. He had planned on becoming a math teacher, but all those plans were canceled. It seemed as if Ernest's life had been planned for him now. He had gotten a job at the local paper mill. He went to work early in the morning and came home late in the afternoon. He had to take care of his wife and baby. Mr. Boone did not have any problems reminding him of that.

I looked at Tom and smiled. I told him that Ernest was a good-looking guy, but it did not matter now because he had taken someone else's hand. Tom agreed and said, "Maybe I can take someone's hand too." I looked at him and said, "Let's see." After eating his cake and drinking his tea, he asked me if I wanted to walk down the street. He yelled out to my father and told him that we were going to walk down the street. My father said okay. I think he liked Tom. He was the first boy that he had let come to the house to see me. Melvin had asked one time, and my father told him to ask the next year. I think that was it for Melvin; he never asked again.

Tom was a nice guy. He was the kind of guy that was almost perfect, but I did not like him. He was tall and dark skinned, with brown eyes and a nice looking body, and he was sweet. He spent some of his time lifting his father's weights. He said his father wanted to be a bodybuilder, but that dream never came true. I knew lots of girls would love to have him, but I did not want him. He was a gentleman at all times. He was smart too. He had finished high school and was working with Mr. Lee at the steel mill shop. He was not just a regular hand, but he was in the office. He knew a lot. Sometimes he would run the shop when Mr. Lee had to go home or go to another town and pick up supplies. All of the workers liked Tom. It seemed as if everybody did. Even the children loved him and looked up to him. His brothers and sister adored him. My cousins loved him and always wanted to be around him. My brothers and sisters loved him. Everybody loved him; I did not love him. I was flattered that he liked me. I was glad to know that I caught his eye, but I just didn't like him. I believe I had fallen in love with Ernest. We had never been together, but I think I had fallen in love with him. I daydreamed about him all the time, but I knew my daydreaming days were over now.

After the walk, Tom told me it was time for him to go. He hugged me and said good night. He ran into the living room and told my parents good night. He told them that if it was okay, he would love to come back on Sundays and see me. They both said okay. Sunday nights came, and week by week I saw Tom. He was nice. I did not have any other interests, so I started looking forward to the visits. We sang in the choir together. We would talk at church and go to the church outings together. Everyone knew we were dating. Everybody knew Tom cared a great deal for me. After nine months of dating, everyone was waiting for him to propose except me. I enjoyed being around him, but I did not love him. Tom wrote me poems; he told me how much he loved me; he told me he wanted to marry me. He was always giving me gifts and always telling my parents how much he cared for me. My brothers and sisters started calling him brother-in-law. I did not want to get married, even though I was getting older. I knew he wanted children because he always talked about what he would do with his sons and how he would protect his daughters. I did not know how to tell him that I did not want to marry him. I wanted a life with a man, but not Tom.

Everyone was excited that the church outing had been changed to July 4th. That was a good time because everyone that had relatives out of town would be home for the holiday. Rev. Jack, the assistant pastor, planned it that way so that the church budget would be met. Tom and I help decorate the grounds. Rev. Jack had everything. He had games for the children, something for the older people, and something for the teenagers. He was excited and happy. He was always looking at me, asking me if I was ready. I would smile and act as if I did not know what Rev. Jack was talking about.

It took us two weeks to get everything ready for the big event. Everyone was doing something. Mrs. Sara was baking cakes, a lot of the older women were cleaning up the church, the men were making sure the bushes and lawn were cut. Rev. Jack said that this was going to be the best event ever.

That day had finally come. Everyone was at church eating, hugging, drinking soda, laughing, talking, etc. I could not wait for this event to be over. I was tired of Tom. If I moved, he moved. He kept looking at me, smiling. I would smile back, but I was ready to go home. As things started coming to an end, I began to feel happy knowing that in a matter of minutes I would be home. Tom continued to smile at me and finally whispered in my ear that it was time. I looked at him and asked him, "What did you say?" Before he could answer, he ran over to my father and started talking to him. After talking to my father for about fifteen minutes, I saw my father shake his hand. My father walked him in the direction of my mother. He talked to her for about ten minutes. All three of them walked in my direction. As they approached me, I looked at them wondering what was going on. As my father got closer, he said that he had told Tom yes. I asked him what he was talking about. At that time, Tom was asking me to marry him. I looked at Tom and all of the other people that had followed him, and I said yes. It happened so fast, I did not know what to say. Tom was the happiest man in the world. He grabbed me and hugged me. He hugged my parents, his parents, and everybody else that was standing around us. I was a bit in shock because I had just made a commitment that I was not happy about. I think I was the saddest person in the world. As Tom hugged people and people hugged me I thought about all of the ways I could have said no. I was wondering to myself if it was too late to change my answer. My mother came to me and said, "It will be alright; no matter what you are feeling, time will change your heart." I looked at her; she smiled and walked away. All of a sudden, I wondered if my mother knew what I was feeling. As Tom and everyone celebrated, I started thinking about having Tom's children. I was so miserable. I wanted to dig a hole in the ground and get in it. Everyone was happy; people had started the fireworks, people were singing, and dancing. Everyone was having a ball but me.

Tom was drunk with happiness. He was running around, smiling. Then all of a sudden, he ran back to me and put a ring on my finger. It was a nice ring. I know Tom must have spent all of his money on the ring. It was beautiful. All of the ladies were running to me to see the ring. They were telling me that Tom was a good man. They were saying that he would make a good father and a good husband. Everyone had something positive to say. Negativity had taken over my brain. All I could do was smile and think of the worse.

I had decided to be Tom's wife, and my parents and Tom were telling everybody. I heard someone ask Tom when we were getting married, and he said the fourth Sunday in September in this church. I almost fainted. It was July, and September was two months away. The older women came and hugged me. Some looked at me and smiled. Others said I hope you know what you are doing and still others said it is a big change, but you will get used to it; we survived.

That evening when I got home, my mother called me into her room. She told me that she wanted the best for me and she thought Tom was a good man. She said that I would not have any trouble with my marriage as long as I allowed Tom to be the man. I just looked at her. She did not say another word. She just walked quietly out of the room. I followed her into the living room. She looked at me and said that she would make me a white dress. She said that she saw Tom making all of the arrangements with Rev. McCarthy. My mother looked at me and said, "Be happy and thank God that you are getting married."

August flew by, and September came quickly. I was still unhappy, but I knew I was going to go along with all of the plans. It was a lot to do. I tried on the white dress twice, and my mother took me shopping to buy my shoes. Tom said he was going to wear one of his father's suits. Everyone was so happy. They were getting ready for this wedding. I would go to church every Sunday and listen to the people congratulate me on the big day. They would say, "You don't have long now." Tom was always standing beside me with a grin on his face nodding saying, "Just a couple of more days, and she will be Mrs. Jenkins." I was trying with everything I had to like him, but it was not happening.

The last Sunday before the wedding, Tom came by the house with some big news. He called my parents around and told them that he wanted to share the good news with everybody. I just listened because I did not know what he was going to say. He said that he had already told his parents, so he wanted to tell my parents and me. I just looked at him with a half grin on my face and asked him to share the news. He said that Mr. Bob Allen called him in his office and told him how pleased he was with his work. He said that Mr. Allen said that his business would not be as successful if it were not for him. He told him that he was happy to hear that he was getting married and he could not wait to meet his bride. I asked Tom to continue. It seemed as if he was taking all day to tell whatever he had to say. He finally yelled out that Mr. Bob Allen was going to let him rent one of his houses. Tom said he immediately asked about the one on Raleigh Lane. He said Mr. Allen said that was the same one he was thinking of. Tom jumped, grabbed me, and said, "We have a house." I smiled. My parents were so happy. Tom said he had more good news. He said that Mr. Allen said if he paid the rent on time for six months, he would let him buy the house. Tom laughed and said we have a house because I have already made arrangements for Mr. Allen to take the money out of my pay. Tom told my father that the yard was so big. He said that he was thinking about having a garden and making space for the children to play. My father just smiled and said, "I know you are going to be a good father and husband."

September 27th finally arrived. I woke up that morning sick. I felt so bad. My head was hurting, my stomach was hurting, and I felt nauseous. I was also scared and mad. I realized that I had to marry Tom. Mom and Dad looked at me and told me I had to get better. My father said, "Don't disappoint Tom. He is a good man and I want you to be a good wife like your mother." My mother said she was going to prepare breakfast. She told me to rest a while, take a shower, then come down to breakfast. I finally got myself together and walked into the kitchen. All of my sisters and brothers had already eaten. I really did not have an appetite. My mother was washing dishes. She asked if I wanted breakfast. I told her that I did not want to see any food. She told me that I was a little nervous, and in a matter of minutes, everything would be over. My mother looked at me and told me to go get dressed. She said that my clothes were on the bed, and everything had been pressed and laid out for me. She told me that she had packed my clothes also. I just looked at her. She reminded me that I would not be home that afternoon. She said that she would send my father to get my clothes. I went to my room to get dressed. I felt empty. I was hurting inside. I held back the tears. I knew then that it was too late. My father knocked on the door, picked up my suitcase, and smiled.

As I sat in the back room, I heard Rev. Jackson tell everyone to take their seats. He said the wedding would start soon. I heard the music and then my father walked into the room. He said that Tom really looked handsome. I don't remember a lot. I remember my father walked me down the aisle. I noticed everyone was standing up. I remember Rev. McCarthy asking me to repeat after him and I remember Tom's brother handing him the ring. Tom reached over and kissed me, and everyone applauded. I don't even remember giving Tom his ring, but when I looked down, he had one on. I did not even purchase the ring. Tom paid for everything. We were starting a marriage and I was not sure if we had money. As I stood there, I realized I had not even thought about this marriage. I knew I would be living with Tom, but what else. I then realized all the things Sally, my cousin in New York, used to talk about when she would come home and talk about her marriage. I got scared, nervous, and felt sick all over again. I looked at Tom and he was smiling at me. I was wondering what was going on in his mind. The only hope I had was that Tom did not know that we had talked about those things. She was the only one that ever talked to me because my mother never talked to me about anything.

We left the church around five o'clock that afternoon, and I got to my house around five thirty. I said goodbye to my parents, and we drove off. I looked back at my mother. She was wiping her eyes. A tear rolled down my eye also. Tom asked me if I was okay. I told him I was fine. He said that he was happy that I was his wife. He said that he only wanted the best for his children and me. I just listened. He said that he knew I did not feel the way he did, but maybe time would change. I looked at him. He said that we never had to talk about what he said, but he just wanted me to know. I looked out of the window until we arrived at the house.

Our house smelled like some kind of disinfectant. Tom's mom had been there for about a week cleaning up. The house was cozy. Everything seemed to have fit in its own corner. I fell in love with the kitchen. The kitchen was bigger than my mother's. It was painted and white curtains hung at the windows. The living room and dining room were beautiful. Tom and his mom had decorated the house. Everything was laid out nicely. The house had three bedrooms upstairs. Our bedroom was the largest. Tom was so excited when he showed me the room. He quickly ran into the other two bedrooms and asked me how I liked the house. He told me that he hoped I liked the house. He told me that the cabinets and refrigerator were full and anything else I needed he would get for me. After that brief discussion, he grabbed my hand and took me back to our bedroom. He asked me how I liked the bedroom. He told me that his mom had picked everything out, but if I wanted it changed, he would buy me what I wanted. He told me that he just wanted everything nice for me. We talked, laughed, hugged, and finally consummated our marriage.

Over the years, I fell madly in love with Tom. He and I had a wonderful marriage, and we had five children. While some of our friends were having problems with their marriages, it seemed as if our marriage got stronger and stronger. Tom got another job and we moved into a larger house. Mr. Allen made sure we got the best deal. We also moved to another section of town. Tom loved our children. He tried to give them everything they wanted. I helped. We tried to make sure they had a great life. My parents and Tom's parents had died, and we were spending a lot of time entertaining my sisters and brothers and Tom's sisters and brothers. It just seemed that we all got along so well. All of our siblings had their own families and careers. All of us were doing well. Our parents would have been proud of all of us.

Life was fun. Marriage was good. We had some setbacks, but we survived. One by one, our siblings started dying. We were always going to funerals. Then Tom died. He went to work, went into his office, sat at his desk, and had a heart attack. I could not believe it. I did not think Tom would die before me. The children were devastated. We all cried until we had no more tears. He was a good man. He was my best friend.

As I sat there thinking, Rodell walked into the room smiling. He wanted to know what I was doing. I told him that I was just thinking about the good times, how I met his father, my in-laws, etc. He asked me if I was ready for the news. I asked him what he was talking about. He said he had asked Tracie to marry him. I looked at him and smiled. Rodell and Tracie grew up together. Tracie was Emma's daughter. Emma and I went to elementary school together. He said that he liked Tracie a lot and he decided that he was not going to let the love of his life go. He said that he wanted to marry her quickly, so they decided to have a private wedding and the reception later. He said that they were going to get married Sunday after church in the pastor's office. I looked at him and reminded him that we only had three days to get everything ready. He said that all plans had been made and all I had to do was be in place. Rodell kissed me and ran out yelling. I laughed and prayed silently to God to keep me until Sunday and then take me because I was ready to go.

Sunday came quickly. At three o'clock in the afternoon, after the service was over, everyone walked to the pastor's office. Rodell rolled me in. I was getting tired of that wheelchair. Everyone in the family came. Rev. Walker was so comical.

Tracie was a beautiful bride. After the wedding, they had a small reception in the cafeteria.

I was so happy that I almost thought about wanting to stay around. I had a ball. It was good to see everybody. I told everyone that I would not be around long. They just looked at me and told me to stop saying foolish things. I welcomed Tracie to the family, and her mom Emma and I talked about how beautiful they looked. I told Tracie if Rodell was anything like his father, she would be madly in love with him in a couple of weeks. She looked a little puzzled, but smiled and said she sure she would be. Her mom said she did not think she could fall any deeper in love. She said that Tracie was waiting for Rodell to propose years ago.

All of the excitement was wonderful. The reception had moved to my house. I got in bed around ten thirty. I was in a lot of pain. Everyone was still walking in and out of the house. Some of my grandchildren were coming in, giving me goodnight kisses and saying goodbye. I continued telling them that I would be leaving. Around eleven o'clock, Rodell came into the room. He said that he and Tracie were leaving. I told him that I wanted to have prayer. We prayed. I told Rodell that the house was his and everything I owned. He smiled. I asked him if he thought Tracie would love the house. I told him that they did not have to stay in their apartment long; they could move into this house. Rodell told me to get a good night sleep. He asked me how I felt. I told him the pain was getting worse and I did not have the strength to go on. I told him that I was sure that I would be leaving soon. He told me to rest. He said that he would lock up and see me in the morning. I told him to always pray and put God first in his life. He said okay and left.

One o'clock in the morning I opened my eyes. I looked around the room and called out to God. I told Him I was ready. I said I had a good life and that He had blessed me more than I could imagine. I ask God to take care of my family, especially Rodell and his new wife. I closed my eyes.

Lost Love, But Not Forgotten

I met him one day in the cafeteria at graduate school. When I first saw him, I felt there was only one thing that we could share, and it was not his lunch. I looked at him with lust in my eyes and heart. I asked my friend if she knew him since she was "Ms. Popular" on campus. She knew everyone. She even knew the freshmen. She said she did. I asked her to introduce us. She started the introduction, and I finished. I told him a little about myself, where I was from, and what I enjoyed doing for fun. As we continued the conversation, I realized that he was in one of my classes. Immediately, I told him that I was having problems in that class and asked if he would come by before class and help me with some things I did not understand. I commended him on how he participated and answered all of the questions correctly. He blushed and said that he would be glad to help me. I gave him my room number and told him where I lived. He wrote down the information and told me that he would see me later that afternoon.

I waited patiently, but he never showed up. Anger was not the word to describe how I felt. I don't think there was a word created to express my feeling. I was upset with him. I could not wait to see him in class and tell him how I felt about him and other men like him.

I had already thought of the names I would call him. I didn't care if it would hurt his feelings. I didn't know if I would wait for the break. I probably would walk right in the class, see him, and start telling him how I felt. I didn't care who heard me or what anyone said. He had messed with the wrong person.

When I walked into the classroom, he was the first one I saw. I walked over to my seat, looked at him, rolled my eyes, and listened attentively as the professor went over the new assignment. I prayed that the break would come quickly so I could give him a "piece of my mind." He would never forget me nor my words when everything was over. I was going to make sure of that. I was not just one of those women he could take for granted.

Break time finally came. It seemed slower than usual. The professor dismissed the class for fifteen minutes. I thought to myself that that was all I needed. I could possibly tell him what I thought in ten minutes. I looked around, but he had rushed out to get water. I walked up to the water fountain and began to explode. I called him a liar. I told him he was full of hot air; he was no good; he was full of himself; he was like other men; and if he didn't want to be bothered, then he should have been man enough to tell me face-to-face. I told him that I expected more from him, but all dogs have similar characteristics no matter how good they look and smell. He looked at me and asked me what I was talking about. I laughed and told him that he could continue playing his crazy game. I told him that I was going back to class. He told me to wait. I turned around and looked at him and shook my head. He said that he was not lying. He told me that he was at the gym lifting weights, and when he noticed the time, it was time for class. He said he was waiting to explain everything in class, but I walked in and sat someplace else. He said he had no intention of hurting me. He apologized. I apologized also. He said that he would see me the next day at the same time. I smiled and said okay.

The class was so boring. I spent most of my time thinking about him and what we would talk about. He was tall. He was about 6'3." He looked as if he weighed between 220-240 pounds, and he was nothing but muscle. His complexion was dark and smooth; he did not have a lot of hair on his face but a thin layer of hair that encircled his top lip. He was so good looking. Everything about him looked good to me. He smelled good, and his clothes fitted him perfectly.

The next day was very sunny and warm. I kept thinking about how he would look and what he would have on. Two o'clock came so slowly, but it finally came. He was fifteen minutes late. He knocked on my door. I answered quickly. He said that he would wait in the lobby. I told him that I was in graduate school, and he was allowed to come into the room. He laughed and said that he did not mind waiting in the lobby. I said okay and told him that I would be there shortly.

I walked next door and almost fainted. He had on a gray sweatsuit that fitted him nicely. I just stared at him, thanking

God silently for molding this man so perfectly. He said hello and I smiled at him and responded. I asked him how his day had been. He said everything was fine. He said he had been to the gym and the library. He asked me what I had been doing. I told him that I had an okay day, but it had gotten better now that he was in the room. We both laughed. He said that he was not going to repeat yesterday. He again apologized for not coming back. I told him that everything had been forgotten and forgiven. I asked him about our class, where he attended undergraduate school, where he was from, what were his plans for the future, his major, his age, how many siblings he had, his middle name, etc. He answered all of my questions. Then he had a list of questions for me. I answered all of them. So far, the most important answers were: he was two years older and intelligent. I braced myself and asked the big question. I asked him about his girlfriend. He said they had just broken up. I was so happy to hear that, but I told him that I was so sorry. He asked me about my boyfriend. I told him that I was talking to a guy, but we were just friends, and I was not in love with him. I also told him that I was not serious about the guy, and anyday, our relationship would be over. I even told him that the guy got on my nerves almost all the time. He looked at me and said, "Please don't hurt him." He told me to be honest with him. He said by not telling him, I would hurt him forever.

I looked at him and wondered why that mattered to him, but I said okay. I told him I would tell the guy the truth soon.

He asked me if I would promise to take care of this issue immediately. I told him I would. He said, "Okay, because I just got dumped by my girlfriend." I looked at him. He smiled and asked me if I would be his friend. I said that I would. He walked over to me and embraced me tenderly. His touch did more than he could imagine. I pulled away from him and the lust that I once felt seemed to have evaporated. It just left. He seemed so sincere and sweet. His concern about someone else just caused me to respect and appreciate him even more. I felt so safe with him. I liked just being in his presence. I made up my mind at that moment that if something was bothering him, I would be there for him, no matter what the problem. I could not believe that someone or something could upset such a gentle soul. I also decided that I would be a friend to him forever. He said he had to go. He walked away, and I left the lobby feeling as if I had been reunited with a lost long friend.

The girls on the hall were waiting to hear the news. I had told them about this man, and they were waiting to hear everything. I walked out and said, "Forget it, nothing happened." They looked at me and asked if I felt okay. They also asked what happened to all of the charm I said I was going to put on him. I smiled and told them that that didn't happen. They looked at me and asked if I needed romance lessons. I laughed, and so did they. They asked me how I let that good-looking man slip through my hands. I told them that I would just take one step and one day at I time. They laughed, and

I walked to my room. I deserved everything they did to me. I bragged to them about all that I would do, but I did nothing. I had to smile to myself.

Thinking about him became rather exhausting. I could not get this man off my mind. I thought about our conversation, how he looked, and the girl that broke his heart. I could not wait to see her. I was almost sure she did something to hurt him. I wondered what kind of person she was and how could she have done such a bad thing. I thought so much about him that I could barely sleep. I dozed and was awakened by my roommate. She wanted to know everything the other girls wanted to know. She was not in the dormitory when I told the other girls the story. She laughed too. I got up and got dressed for bed. I told her good night. She was still laughing. I finally fell asleep thinking about seeing him the next day.

Morning came quickly. I jumped up, showered quickly, and rushed to the cafeteria before the breakfast line closed. I had gotten accustomed to eating breakfast every morning, so if I missed breakfast, it seemed that my whole day was unorganized. I walked in and to my amazement, I saw him. He was getting his breakfast. He saw me and smiled. He asked where I was sitting, and I told him to pick a table. I could not get my breakfast fast enough. This guy, in just two days, had become the most interesting thing on the planet. We talked over breakfast and spent almost three hours in the cafeteria. I was just thankful to God that I was in graduate school and had all evening classes. If not, I would have missed my morning classes and would not have cared. Nothing was as important as this time. He talked about his family, his life, his goals, undergraduate school, his love for football, and me. We left the cafeteria, and he said he would stop by later. That stop became routine. He came by every day after that, and I became more and more interested in him. Even though he enjoyed my company and I enjoyed his, it seemed as if he had something else on his mind. I did not want to ask him too many questions about his personal life. I was concerned. I was concerned about his break up and the girl that caused him so much pain.

He was the same way in class. He would be very involved in the discussion. It seemed as if he would drift off into something else. The same thing would happen when we took walks. We would start off talking and laughing about how far we would walk and then he would get quiet. This went on for a while, and then one day, he told me something was bothering him, and he felt that he needed to share it with me. I was honest with him and told him that I thought something was on his mind. I told him how I had noticed that he seemed as if something was bothering him. He told me that he had been talking to his girlfriend. He said she wanted him to come by and see her. He said that she had apologized and wanted to start the relationship over. I did not want him to go. I feared the relationship would start again. For once in my life, I felt I had something that was workable. I felt we had a good thing going, and that eventually, it would grow into something bigger than I could imagine. I did not want to lose what we had started. I told him not to go and to try to forget the past. I told him that just seeing her would bring back the pain. He listened and said that he was going because he needed to talk to her. He said that he needed to give her an opportunity to explain what happened. I told him that her actions explained what happened. He told me that she was a good young lady. He said that they had gone together off and on for about five years. I reminded him that an off and on relationship was trouble. He told me that everything I said was correct, but he had to give it another try. He said he was hurt, but he wanted to give her an opportunity to make everything alright. I got so angry with him. I stopped talking. I told him to do what he felt was right. He said that he had decided to go and that he would be back around eleven. He asked me to wait up for him. I told him I would, but deep down inside, I knew I was lying. I could not believe that he was asking me to stay awake to hear him tell how he and his woman had gotten back together.

Since he would spend time with his past, I would too. He left that afternoon with a promise that he would see me later that evening. I left him knowing that I was going to telephone an interest of mind that I met six months ago.

My interest was a nice guy. He would come by and see me periodically. He was not my ideal guy at all. He was different than the other guy I was dating, but neither one of them would be the man that I wanted to walk beside the rest of my life. I told him about my new friend. He called him 6 Feet. I would talk about 6 Feet all the time when I was with him. He would listen and tell me to let him go. He would tell me that he would eventually go back to his girlfriend. He would tell me that no matter what his girlfriend did, she would always have a place in his heart. I guess he was right. I should have known that information myself but I guess I was so naïve. I guess I thought he was different.

I telephoned Monte. He seemed as if he was glad to hear from me. I told him I wanted to go out and have fun. I told him that I did not want to think about anything; I just wanted to have a good time. He asked me about my friend (6 Feet). I told him that he was on his way to see his girlfriend. Monte laughed and told me that he knew this would happen. He asked me what time did I want him to come by. I told him it did not matter. I was just sitting in my room, passing the time away. He said that he would pick me up and we could go to dinner.

I spent most of the time talking about him. After dinner, Monte could not keep his hand off me. He kept kissing me on my hand, my neck, and my forehead. I told him that I had to go. He asked me to spend more time with him that night. I told him that I had some studying to do. Monte was not in college and had never been. He would always talk about what he would have done with a college degree. He would tell me how proud he was of all of my accomplishments. He would talk about how happy he would be to be in the audience when I got my graduate degree. He said he understood how important studying was so he would call me later. He told me that since my friend would be out of my life, we could spend more time together. He took me home, kissed me on the cheek. I thanked him for understanding and for spending time with me. He was nice, but I missed my new friend.

I watched television for the rest of the evening and ate everything in sight. I went to bed. Around eleven o'clock that night I heard the doorbell ring. I did not move. All of a sudden, there was a knock on the door. I told the person to come in. It was Dawn, the girl down the hall. She told me that my male friend was downstairs. She said he was waiting for me to come down. I looked at her. She looked at me and asked if I were getting up. I told her to tell him that she knocked but I did not answer. I told her to tell him that I was asleep. She asked me what was wrong. I just looked at her and asked her to deliver the message. She said okay. She left my room and walked down the stairs. She came back quickly and said that he said okay.

I thanked her for her help. She looked at me and smiled and told me not to let him get away. She said some people look a lifetime to find "Mr. Right." I again thanked her and told her that I would think about what she said. She said okay. I got up, looked out of the window, and saw him crossing the street. Even in the dark, he looked magnificent. I should have gone downstairs to see him, but my pride and anger would not allow me to do so.

The next morning, I met him at breakfast in the cafeteria. He was quiet and asked me about my evening and night. I told him that I studied and fell asleep. He became very angry. He started talking about unfaithful women and how he could not understand them. He talked about how they say one thing and do another. He talked about how they go out and come back with marks on their necks and those marks indicate what happened and how they spent their evening or night. I smiled and wondered what he was talking about. I wondered why he was so upset. I thought that maybe his girlfriend had really ended the relationship. I again asked him if he was okay. He said he was okay. He asked me if I was okay. He looked so angry. I looked at him. I asked him about his friend. He said that she was okay. I asked him if they had made plans to rekindle their relationship. He looked at me and said no. He asked me if I had ended all of my relationships. I did not know what was wrong with him. I thought that he and his girlfriend must have had a big argument. I hated to see him that way, but I was glad to know that his relationship was over. I asked him did he think he and his girlfriend would continue being friends. He told me once he said it was over, it was over. He said that he did not say one thing, lie, and say something different. He said the people who you trust the most hurt you the most. I just looked at him. I told him that I was sorry about what he had to go through. I told him that if I could, I would give his girlfriend a lecture on how to treat a good man. He asked me if I knew what a good man was or looked like. I looked at him and smiled. I told him that I was sorry about what happened, but he seemed as if he was taking some of his anger and hurt out on me. He said I was right. He said he had a right to get upset with me. He said that he had some things to deal with, and he had learned to accept people for the decisions they make. He said he had to accept that. I looked at him and felt this woman must have really damaged his self-esteem. He said that he had to go. He got up quickly, knocked the chair over, poured his milk in his plate, and said he would see me later. He left me sitting at the table. He put his plate in the trash. He turned to me, waved, and said I will see you later.

I went back to my room, puzzled. I was angry to know that this woman had hurt him so badly. I just wanted to know what she was like and what kind of hold he had on this man. I was tired of thinking about it, so I decided to take a nap. I slept for about two hours. I woke up feeling so tired that I knew that a shower was the only thing that would wake me up. I grabbed my towel and jumped in. The water felt so good and relaxing. While I was drying off, I noticed my neck. I was shocked. I had marks all over my neck. I thought about Monte and how he was kissing me on my neck. I had no idea this had happened. I was shocked. I was so embarrassed. This was what he was talking about. He was talking about me. I felt so foolish. All the time, I thought he was talking about his girlfriend. He was talking about me. I was so hurt. Even though he never talked about starting a relationship, I knew then that those marks affected him. I knew he thought I was just like his girlfriend. I had messed up whatever we had. I knew I was falling in love with him, and if he was feeling the same way, I destroyed everything. I felt like a fool. How could I want something so badly, possibly get it, and turn around and mess it up? I got my clothes on and ran over to his house. He was not home. I saw Glenda, who lived in my dormitory. She was visiting her boyfriend. Her boyfriend and my friend rented a room in the same house. I told her what had happened. She told me that she was sure everything would be okay. I told her to tell him I stopped by. She said she would. I also left a note on his door.

Later on that night, he stopped by to see me. He told me that he had gotten the note and that Glenda told him I came by. He looked depressed. I asked him if he was okay, and he said he was feeling a little down. I asked him if he was upset with me. I did not know what to do. I apologized. I told him the whole story. He listened. He seemed so upset. He told me that he understood. He told me how it made him feel when he saw those marks on my neck. I told him that I did not know they were there. He told me that his relationship was over, and he wanted to tell me about it that night. I told him that I was sorry, but my anger about him going to see his girlfriend had gotten the best me. He looked at me and said, "You have to trust me. I will tell you what I am thinking, what I am feeling, and what I am going to do." He grabbed my hand, dropped it, and said that he had to go. He said he needed some time to think; I just looked at him. I asked him if he wanted to go to the church down the street because they were having a revival. I told him that maybe he could hear something to make him feel better. He asked me if I wanted to go with him. I told him no, but maybe he could go there and feel better. He said he thought that was a good idea. He kissed me on my forehead. He said that he thought he would give church a try. Since I did not feel I was the biggest sinner in the world, I felt I could give church a break for a while. He left.

I had a lot of school work to do so I quickly got started on my assignments. I tried not to think about him. I hoped that he would hear something in church that would help him forgive me and his ex-girlfriend. I did not want to think about what problems and the additional pain I had caused him. I just hoped that something he would hear in church would help our relationship. I knew most people got an answer when they went to church, and hopefully, he would get one too. If not, I would just accept that whatever happened was my fault.

That night around eleven o'clock, someone knocked on my door. I was just finishing up my last assignment. I opened the door, and he walked in. He had a big smile on his face. I smiled back and asked him about the church service. He told me it was great. He said that God had changed his life. He told me that he had accepted God in his life and that he would live his life forever serving and pleasing Him. I looked at him and said okay. I did not know what to do. I wanted him to go to church, but I was not expecting him to come back with that news. It was good that God changed his life, but what did this mean for us. I just looked at him. He continued to tell me about his new experience. I listened. My roommate was not in, so he sat on her bed. He just kept telling me about his experience. He could not thank me enough. We watched television almost all night. We both fell asleep. I was on my bed, and he was on my roommate's bed. Around six o'clock in the morning, he jumped up. I laid quietly in bed, wondering what he was going to do. He got up and walked over to my bed. He bent down and kissed me on my forehead. I looked up at him and smiled, and he said he had to go. He smelled so good. I just stared at him. I asked him why he was leaving. He smiled and said, "I am going to prove to you that I am not like other guys." He said that God wanted him to respect me and treat me like a lady. I smiled at him and sighed at the same time. I could not believe he had gone to church, and as he said, God changed his life. He looked at me and walked out of the door. He said that he would see me later. I heard him as he walked down the steps. I heard the door open and slammed. I ran to the window and saw him cross the street. I was so in love with him. As I continued to watch him, I wondered again and again what this change in his life meant for me.

He loved going to church. He was in church all the time. He tried hard to get me to go. I went a couple of times, but I was not ready to make that serious commitment. I would go only to be with him. He came by to see me every day, but most of his evenings were in church. We had good times. I felt he loved me too, but we never talked about that. He was a man true to his word. He treated me like a lady at all time. Even when I felt he wanted to get close to me, he fought his feelings, pushed me away, and started talking about his relationship with God. He would tell me that no one could make him break his relationship with God.

47

He came by early one morning to tell me what he thought was good news. He told me that he was leaving the university. He said that he was not happy being in school, so he wanted to work for a while. He said he would visit and keep in touch. He kissed me on the cheek and said goodbye. He said he would call once he got settled. I asked him where he was going. He said he was not sure, but he would know when he got there. He told me that he would be okay. He told me that he would come back and visit the church and he would come back and visit me. I held back the tears. It seemed as if a lump developed in my throat and I could not swallow for hours. I sat on the bed. I could not believe what had happened. I could not believe that he walked out of my room and my life. I did not know what was going on. For almost four months, this man had been everything to me. I saw him every day. We ate at least one meal together. We laughed, talked, watched television, and I even went to church with him a couple of times. I could not believe he left me. Finally, I had met the man of my dreams and he was gone; he left my life. I felt like a piece of my heart was bleeding. I could not believe that this good man had not only left me but my heart.

Days passed and I did not hear from him. Since we had not made any serious commitment to each other, I started dating again. I was going out, having fun, and enjoying life to the fullest. I still missed him, and I was very lonely. I missed the times we spent together, our talks, our walks, and just being with him. I was not sure what he was doing, but all I knew was that he was not with me. I wanted to talk to him. I wanted to laugh with him. I wanted to ask him about his job and what plans he had made for his life. I wanted to know if I were in those plans, and if not, who was fortunate enough to be the woman in his life. I wanted to see his smile. I was going out and had met another male friend, but I spent a lot of my time thinking about him and talking about him to anyone who would listen. He was on my mind all the time.

Glenda said he had come by several times, but I was unaware of his visits. During these times, I was out with friends or off campus. I was busy. I stayed gone a lot. If I was not out with my friend, I was out with my roommate. We had become very good friends. I think she knew I was having a hard time dealing with the separation. We would do almost everything together. I would visit her parents on the weekend, and we would have such good times. Her parents treated me just like their child. I think she had told them what I was going through with my friend. I know her mother knew because she would always have talks with me about moving on and not getting stuck in the past. She would tell me that the future had so much to offer, but if I stayed in the past, I would never see it. She was right and I would always listen to her.

One Sunday, when I was coming back with my roommate, I saw him. He was leaving his brother's dormitory. His brother lived in the undergraduate dormitory about ten minutes from where I lived. She stopped the car and I got out. I called him. He looked back and ran over to me. I asked him if he had been by to see me, and he said no; he needed to see his brother. He said he had to talk to him about family business. He said he would be back soon. He asked me if I had been going to church. I told him no. He told me that I should visit sometimes. He walked to his car, got in, and waved bye. He pulled off. I could not believe what had happened. My roommate looked at me and said, "You need to move on with your life because I think he has moved on with his." I thought about what she said, but I wondered why he was visiting his brother and why he was in such a hurry to leave. Even though his brother was on the same campus, I never asked him questions about his family or his life. I had been introduced to him, and when I saw him, I would speak and smile; he would do the same. I again wondered what that visit was about and why he didn't stop by to see me or why was he in such a hurry to leave. I guess I had to let that fantasy go.

Weeks had gone by, and I had not heard from him or seen him. I had just given blood on campus (anytime the blood bank came, you could depend on me) and for some reason, I was feeling cold. All I could think about was wrapping up in my favorite blanket. I ran to the dormitory. When I walked upstairs, he was standing in front of my door. I invited him in and we talked for hours. We talked about his job, but most of his attention was on me. From that day, I knew I had to tell him how I felt. I loved him. I was not the most faithful person when he was away, but I loved him. After he left that night, I told my roommate that I had to tell him how I felt. She said I should tell him. I wanted to, but I did not know how he would feel or what he would say. My days and nights were spent thinking about him. I missed him when he was away. His visits were getting farther and farther apart.

He left that night, and it was almost five weeks before I saw him again. I called him several times, but he was out running errands for his supervisor. He was all I could think of. I knew that sooner or later, I would have to tell him about my feelings. I knew I had to accept whatever answer he would give me; I had to get it off my chest.

I was coming from the university bookstore when I fell and twisted my ankle. I did not see that hole. I had never experienced pain like that before. I went home, got in bed, and stayed in bed that afternoon and the next day. The pain was worse the next day. I could not bear it anymore, so I had one of my friends drive me to the doctor. Thank God he was a big man because he almost had to lift me up to get me down the stairs. We made it to the doctor. The doctor was not shocked to hear what had happened. He said he expected me to feel that pain and even more. He told me that a bone in my foot was pressing against another bone. He said that what was causing the pain and I needed surgery immediately. He told me that if I did not get it corrected, I would possibly be in pain forever. I did not know what to do. I did not give the doctor an answer. I went home and talked to my roommate. She did not know what to say or tell me what to do. I did not have time to have surgery, and I did not want to be out of school for an extended period of time. I wrestled with all those thoughts and finally fell asleep.

When I woke up, he and my roommate were standing over me. I looked shocked and asked him why he was there. He told me he stopped by, and my roommate had told him what had happened. Immediately, I began telling him how I could not have surgery and how I did not want to leave school. I told him, I did not know how long it would take me to heal and how I wanted to graduate on time. He looked at me; he appeared to be concerned about me and my foot. He wrapped my foot and told me that he would take care of me. In the back of my mind, I was glad I was in pain. I knew that he would be with me until I got better. He was a caring man. I believed with all my heart that he would not leave until I felt better. He said that he was going to church and wanted me to go with him. I just looked at him, maybe I was wrong about him being around. I had to understand that nothing came between him and God. I looked at him and told him I would go. He smiled and said he knew the pain would leave now. I just smiled.

Based on his responses, I am sure it was a great sermon. At the end of the service, he asked me if I was still in pain. I told him I was. He told me that he wanted me to meet the minister. I looked at him strangely, but I said okay. We walked to the back of the church. He introduced me to his minister. He asked me my name and if this was my first time visiting the church. I told him that I had been there before. He told me that I was with a nice guy, and he talked about how faithful he was in coming to church and assisting with whatever they asked him to do. Before the minister finished talking, he told him about my foot. The minister looked down and saw it was wrapped. He asked me what was wrong, and I told him what the doctor said. He asked me if I wanted him to pray for my foot. I did not know what to say, so I said yes. He asked us to join hands, and he prayed. I did not know what to do, so I just stood there until he stopped.

I thanked him and we left. We went back home in silence. Finally, he broke the silence by asking me how I felt. I told him I felt okay. He promised me that the pain would leave. I did not say anything. He walked me to the door and hugged me like never before and pushed me away from him. I looked him straight in his eyes and said good night. He told me that he would be spending the night in town. He told me that he would come by in the morning after breakfast. The more I saw him, the more I knew I was falling deeper and deeper in love. I had been telling my girlfriend Joan everything about him. Joan was from my hometown. She would do pop up visits every now and then. She enjoyed college life. Even though I did not see her every day, she was truly a good friend. I could tell her anything. She would always listen and give you the right advice; she never used it for herself. She knew that I was in love with him because I talked to her about him all the time. I had never experienced this feeling before. I had boyfriends before, but none of them made me feel this way. He was such a great gentleman. He was respected and admired by almost all of the churchgoers. When I would go to church with him, I used to look at him and imagine our wedding, our children, and our home. No man had ever interested me enough for me to think about me having children. He was just all of that to me. He was the man that every little girl dreamed of marrying one day.

I guess Joan got tired of me talking but. you could not tell if she did or didn't. She always received me with an open ear. I knocked on her door to give her more information about him. I talked and talked about him until she told me that she would talk to him. She reminded me that she knew him before me and that they were good friends. She also reminded me that she was the one that introduced us. She said that she would let him know how I felt. She said that maybe it would be better for someone else to tell him. She said that she understood how difficult and awkward it would be, but she would make sure he got the true story. She also said she was tired of me telling everyone how much I loved him and how I was going to tell him one day. She said that she was going to intervene and put an end to my wondering. She told me that I needed to get an answer so that I could move on with my life. I told her that she was right. I thanked her. I felt if I could not tell him, maybe someone else would tell him. Joan was the one. I knew she would do a good job. She told me that she would tell him at breakfast the next time he appeared in the school cafeteria, although he had moved from campus. Sometimes when he would come to visit, if he got there early enough, he would eat breakfast in the cafeteria.

I had a restless night. I thought about Joan telling him. I thought of how happy he would be to hear the news and then

I thought he would smile and tell me the next time he saw me that we could only be friends. I thought that maybe he would tell me that he had rekindled that relationship with his ex-girlfriend. I was a mess. I had thought about every scenario, but the final answer would come from him. I fell asleep. I woke up nervous. I knocked on Joan's door but she was gone. I went next door to talk to Glenda. She told me that she thought he liked me a lot. She said that she had watched him when he was near me. She said everything about him indicated that he was in love with me. I smiled and told her I hoped she was right.

The doorbell rang. I looked out the window and saw him. I started trembling immediately. He asked me to open the door. As I ran down the steps, I thought of how I would handle the disappointment. I thought about what kind of facial expression I would use. Of course, I had to act as if it didn't upset me at all. Whatever he said, I knew he would tell the truth. I opened the door. He smiled as always. He asked me how my day was going. He began to talk about breakfast. He gave the cooks a compliment and then said he missed seeing me at breakfast. I told him that I was not feeling well and most of all, I did not know he would be eating breakfast in the cafeteria that morning. I looked at him wondering what had happened. I was sure by now he would have given me negative or positive feedback based on what Joan had told him. I started wondering if Joan had said anything. Maybe Joan was talking to him about something else. After all, they were friends before I met him. Once he finished his statements, I told him to come upstairs.

He followed me. All I could hear was his heavy footsteps as he took step after step. We finally approached my room. He told me that he wanted to sit in the lobby. I said okay and followed him there. I was beginning to get a bit frustrated because nothing was said. Maybe it was a joke to him. Maybe I was not good enough for him. I was good enough to spend time with, but not to love. I was getting tired of this situation anyway. Maybe it was time for this to be over. I had wasted too much time with him. I had to finish my paper, my exams, and get out of this place. That was my new plan. I was going to concentrate on that from now on until graduation.

He laid back in the chair and said he had made a serious decision. Thinking that it involved me, I quickly asked what. He said that he was leaving his job and taking another job three hours away. I could not believe my ears. He was telling me about taking another job and not talking about what Joan had said to him. I looked at him and told him to keep in touch. I asked him if he had made all the necessary arrangements. He said he was moving over the weekend. I asked if he would visit. He said he would. I held back the tears when he came to me and pulled me near him. He told me that I was a true friend and that I truly had made a difference in his life. He smiled and said he had to go home and finish packing. On his way out of the door, he reminded me that he would come back and visit the church on some Wednesday nights. I smiled as he whispered goodbye.

Lost Love, But Not Forgotten

Life had gotten so much better for me. I had met new friends, and life was really looking up for me. I was really enjoying life. My roommate and I were even closer. She was dating a great guy. I called him my brother-in-law. I was not dating, but really concentrating on my school work. I had joined an organization on campus and was spending time going places with some of the members. I was having a ball. Every weekend I was involved with friends. I would get home Sunday afternoon and drag myself in my room because I was so tired. I would put my key in the door and fall on the bed. It was routine. I did the same thing on May 15th, and two minutes later he walked in the door. I was so surprised. I was happy to see him. He stood tall and very handsome at the door. He asked me to come to the lobby with him. Everything I used to feel for him came back. We walked in and sat down. He asked me how I was doing. He said he was concerned about my classes and my week. We talked for a short while. Then he looked at me rather strangely. He got up, pulled me up from my chair, and embraced me. He held me so tightly. He looked at me and told me that he loved me and he had always loved me. I looked at him. For months, I had waited for him to say this. I asked him to tell me what he said, and he repeated the words. He said, "I love you." He smiled and said, "I know you feel the same way." I told him how I felt about him and he told me how he felt about me. We talked for hours. I asked him what was next. He said we had to take one day at a time. He smiled and told me he had to leave.

He told me that this goodbye did not mean forever. He said he would be back. He embraced me tightly, kissed me, and left.

I could not wait to tell my roommate and the girls on the hall. Everyone was so happy for me. The days, weeks, and months had finally worked out in my favor. This was the happiest night of my life, but my night was full of twists and turns. I could not wait to tell everyone I knew about the good news. I had finally gotten the man that I had fallen in love with; the man of my dreams and the man that I knew I could not live without. Life could only offer me the best since I had finally gotten my man.

It was déjà vu. Weeks passed, but I heard nothing. I called him over and over, but there was no answer. I really did not feel he was sick or hurt, I felt he was doing everything in his power to ignore me. He was not even showing up for work. I could not understand. I could not eat. I could not sleep, and worse of all, I could not study. I found myself crying and experiencing pains in my head and heart that were impossible to describe. I was falling behind in my work. I was depressed, frustrated, and sick. I made up my mind that I could not continue going through this. Again, I became totally engrossed in my life. I ended up talking to a therapist to help cope with everything I was going through.

Graduation came. I was the happiest person in the school. I was trying on my cap and gown when he walked in. He congratulated me on my success. I looked at him with one tear in my eye and asked him what the future held for us. He embraced me. He looked at me and told me that I would always be his friend. He told me that he loved me. I smiled and told him that I would always care. I told him that I loved him and would never forget him. I told him that love does not mean never seeing a person. He told me he understood. He began to explain what had happened. I put my finger over his lips and told him that we had to go our separate ways. He looked at me and said he understood.

Fifteen years passed. We had been in contact via telephone and letters, but no fire was rekindled. He now lives hours away from me. Just talking to him sometimes on the telephone caused my heart to beat harder. My last telephone call put the finishing touches on everything. In talking to him, I asked him if there was any hope for us. After fifteen years and in a distant voice, Hogan said, "No." He said he would always care, but I must let go of the dreams. I thanked him for his honesty and told him that I cared. He said he cared also. I told him that I realized that all dreams do not come true.

As I closed the final pages on Hogan and all our memories, I can still say that I loved him very much. The time I shared with him was truly a love that was lost, but it will never be forgotten.

Reality

It was early in the morning when I heard the noise outside. I jumped up and looked out the window. To my amazement, I saw two men standing with two guns and a lady lying on the ground. What was going on? Was that Mrs. Conners? Where was Mr. Conners?

Who were those men? Why was she on the ground? I looked across the street to see if there were people stirring in the neighborhood, but I did not see or hear anyone. I glanced down the street, and I did not see the Johnson's kids. Nelly and Robert Johnson had two kids, and no matter how early in the morning they were always out greeting the people going to work. The people going to work! Where were they? They were always smiling as if going to work was the best thing ever. Just seeing the glow on their faces in the morning brought so much joy and closeness to the community.

I ran out of the bedroom and into the dining room to peep some more and oh my God, there it was. There were eight trucks and about twenty men. All of them were busily pulling, lifting, and pushing bodies. What was this? I was confused and frightened at the same time. As I continued to look, I saw more men with guns standing guard at the truck. I saw many people I knew, and they were all dead. I saw Mr. Royce, Harley Wright, Sara Courts, Lisa, Mr. and Mrs. Bagley, and Randy. Randy was my ex-boyfriend. He was lying on the ground with everyone else.

Blood was everywhere. They were wrapping the bodies up in what looked like large garbage bags. Forgetting that someone could have been watching me, I yelled and began banging on the window. Tears were streaming down my face. The gunmen looked around and I fell quickly to my feet. I did not want them to see me. All I could think about was that Randy was dead. I did not know what was going on. Who would kill Randy? Randy was such a nice man. He always thought that we were meant for each other. He would always talk about us getting married.

I just gave him such a hard time. He loved me, and I knew he did. Now he was dead. I liked him a lot. I was always looking for someone else. I didn't know if he was the one for me, and I was not sure that I wanted to spend the rest of my life with him. He was there for me in my good times and in my bad times. He taught me how to drive, gave me my first real dozen of roses, took me places, showed me the beauty of life, and always respected and treated me like a lady. My friends always thought he was not good enough for me, and I guess I didn't either.

He was always around. He always told me that he just wanted to love me. One day I decided it was over. I could not continue playing with his emotions. He could not understand, but deep inside, I knew I was not in love with him. I just decided that I would see what else life had to offer me. The dating life wasn't all that great. Randy would always call and say he would always be around, and if I were ever in trouble, just call and he would be there for me. I guess I would never have that opportunity. Tears continued to roll down my cheeks. As I wiped them away, I realized that I had probably lost a good man. Even though I felt my life was in danger, I had to keep looking out of the window.

I pulled myself up quietly and I was surprised to see all of the blood on the street. Blood was all over the place. I knew then that everyone in the community was dead. All of a sudden, I heard footsteps. I knew they were coming to get me. I sat quietly on the couch, knowing that in a matter of minutes, I would be dead. The man stood in front of my window and yelled that he felt they had gotten everyone. He said we have all of them. We have accomplished our mission. The trucks started and slowly pulled away. I felt my heart, and it felt as if at any minute, it was going to burst out of me. I felt my blouse. It was wet from my tears. I wept for everyone. I did not know what to do or who to call. I was so frightened. I felt sick. I ran to the bathroom and vomited until nothing came up but water. I felt so weak. I had cried so much that my face was hurting. I sat on the floor and cried again. I just could not believe anything I had just seen. I reached for the telephone to call the police, but there was no dial tone. They had come in this community and cut telephone lines as well as killed everyone they saw. I just could not imagine what this was about and why this happened. Had the community made someone angry?

I just did not know what was going on. I was so tired and scared. I did not know if they would realize that they had not killed everyone and would come back. I did not know whether to leave the house or stay indoors. Fear had really overtaken me. It looked as if the cars were okay.

I did not know where to turn or what to do. I was devastated. I laid against the chair and cried even harder. After sitting for minutes or even hours, I got up and just walked in circles. I looked at myself in the mirror. I looked five years older. I thought about the deaths. I opened the window, and all I could smell was blood, It smelled like raw meat. I again ran to the bathroom. I had gotten sick again. Nothing was in my body. My whole body ached. I was physically and mentally sick. I had to get help. I had to do something.

Our community was small. We were located in the southern part of the country. People had settled in this community years ago. We did not have what the big cities had, but it was modern enough for us. We had our own grocery store, funeral home, bank, discount stores, and gas stations. We also had a post office and a police station. Melvin Fields was the police officer. He did more visiting than anything. We really did not have any crime.

He was usually at one of the discount stores waiting on customers. If he was needed, everyone knew where to find him.

He was such a friendly man. His wife died three years ago, and he had become a ladies' man. All of the widows, and some that were not, were always inviting him over for coffee or preparing meals for him. They said they felt so sorry for him now that Lorraine had gone. It was almost hilarious to see how they were literally running behind him, asking him if he needed anything.

We had telephones, cars, electronics, etc., but we had to go to the big city when we wanted to buy some things. We had a couple of buses that would pick people up almost anywhere and take them to the grocery store. Education was important, but to get it, one had to leave that area. We had one elementary/ middle school, one high school, one recreation center, and one daycare center. We also had churches, but most people went out of the city on Sundays. They would go to churches in the city and sometimes spend the whole day out. They would visit family and have dinner.

When we really wanted to shop, we traveled about two hours from home. We were comfortable, though. We were family. Everybody knew everyone, and we protected each other. As I thought about all of this, I realized my community family was all gone.

I went into the bathroom and washed my face. I undressed and got in the bed, shaking. Night was falling, and I was all alone. I was hoping that someone would come by. The next town was six miles away. I had friends there. I was hoping that maybe someone would think about me and call.

Reality

I thought about Randy. I missed him already. A tear came down. I thought about my parents. They had died about five years ago in a car accident. I thought I would never sleep again when they died. I was at work when I got the telephone call. I remember screaming and falling down on the floor. It seemed as if my whole life had been snatched from me in a moment.

My co-worker surrounded me and asked me what was wrong. I could not speak. My supervisor picked up the telephone and talked to someone. They took me to the hospital. I don't know how many needles they gave me to calm me down. My co-workers were by my side from the time I left the hospital. They planned the arrangements and were with me at the funerals.

I could not go back to work. Life just stopped working for me for a while. I resigned from my job, sold my parents' house, and left. This was the time that I wished for a sister or brother, but I did not have anyone. My cousins were helpful, but I knew that I had to leave.

I moved from the big city to this community. I researched the location and found it to be a quiet, inexpensive place, not a lot of people. This was where I decided to come. I was the new person for a long time, but everyone accepted me. I told a couple of people about my parents' tragic accident, but I am sure they told everyone else. Some of my neighbors would ask if I was okay and how was I adjusting to everything in my life.

As I thought more and more about the people and the terrible incident, I felt bad that I was not able to help them. What could have happened? Why was I spared? Were they coming back to get me? Had they realized that one had escaped? Who could have done such a terrible thing? I kept asking myself these questions over and over. I knew big investors would sometimes come by the police station and ask if the members of the community were interested in selling their homes because they had plans to do something with the property. Melvin would always tell them no. He would say that everyone was happy and content. I wondered if some of them just decided to take our community without our permission. I am not sure what could have happened unless it had something to do with the Radford girl.

The Radford girl incident was supposed to be the "hush story," but everyone knew about it and had heard it over and over again. I heard it about four days after I moved into the community. I will never forget Ms. Thelma. She walked over and said, "Are you the new girl that moved here. Are you the one that left the big city?" I said yes, and she said, "Well, let me tell you something. Don't tell anyone. You are new, and I think you should know this." Then she asked me if I could keep a secret. She said that she would deny telling me if I happened to tell anyone that she told me. I just looked at her and said okay. She suggested that we sit on the bench around the store so nobody would hear or see her talking to me about the story. I followed her around the store. She put her glasses on, took her handkerchief out of her purse, put it on her knees, and started talking. Every now and then, she would take the handkerchief off her knees and fan flies and bees and say, "Bees just love me because I wear such expensive perfume." I just looked and listened.

The story was interesting. Ms. Thelma said that one of the community boys had fallen in love with the Radford girl who lived in the city. She said that the Radfords were wealthy. Mr. Radford, the father, was always on the local television channels talking about his investments, his property, and his daughter. She said he would always say if you wanted to make money you had to be around money. He also talked about how he had convinced his daughter to not even talk to a young man if his family did not have money. He said that he would select the boy for his daughter to marry and interview his family to make sure they had enough money to take care of her. He encouraged other fathers to do the same. Ms. Thelma said that he was always saying stuff on television. She said she would watch him sometimes. She said he seemed nice enough, but sometimes he would talk too much. She said he was generous. He donated money to our schools and other schools in similar communities. He appeared to be a good man, but eventually, the real person came out. She said the Radford girl got pregnant. Richard was the father. He told his parents, and they told him that they would help him take care of the child.

Richard and his family lived in our community. The news spread quickly. He said that he met her one day when he visited the city. They talked, and he would go back to see her. He said that Mr. Radford did not know of this and the two of them and her friends kept the secret. Richard told his parents that he knew he had to tell someone because her weight gain would eventually have someone suspect that she was carrying a child. Richard's parents knew Mr. Radford was going to be angry, but they knew they had to do the right thing. They drove into the city, went by Mr. Radford's house, and told him the news. They said Mr. Radford almost had a heart attack. They said that when the daughter said she was pregnant, he told her to be quiet. He told her that she would not bring this disgrace on his family. He also told her that she would not have this child and he would never accept this from her. He told her he had plans for her life and she would carry them out or else. Richard's parents tried to express their thoughts and feelings, but he ordered them out of his house. Richard did not see her for weeks.

He was afraid that the father would hurt him. He tried calling her friends, but they would not answer. Ms. Thelma said the whole town feared for his life. Three months had passed, and everyone got the news on television. It was a special report. She said that the news reporter sounded as if he wanted to cry when he announced that Wanda Radford was dead. The reporter said that her body was found in a wooded shed near her home. The body was badly beaten and burned. Mr. Radford talked about the incident on television. He said he did not know what happened, and he wanted answers. Ms. Thelma said he did not seem sad at all. He never mentioned her pregnancy. Richard was devastated; he committed suicide the next day.

Everyone thought that Mr. Radford killed his daughter
or had someone to kill her because she was pregnant. The
community thought that he would do anything to keep her
from Richard.

All of a sudden, I realized that thinking about what Ms.
Thelma had told me was getting me more upset. None of
this was making me feel better, so I decided that I had to do
something. I did not know what to do, but I knew that I could
not survive in this deserted, bloody, and smelly community. I
had to go.

I finally pulled myself together and got up. I looked around
the bedroom and in the direction of my bathroom. Everything
looked dim. I felt so empty. I felt so hollow inside. I felt hopeless,
helpless, frightened, and so all alone. I went into the bathroom,
threw water on my face, and just started putting on clothes. I
was so weak. I was hurting inside. I started thinking again.
Who did this? Who did this to us? What happened? How did
this happen? Again, I thought about what I saw. I saw men
holding guns; I saw bodies wrapped in sheets, and blood, blood
everywhere. Oh, it was horrible. I had to get out. I had to
walk in the community. I was not going to knock on any doors
because I knew everybody was dead.

What if the gunmen came back? Well, that was a chance I
had to take. I made up my mind. If they were out there, I would
die. I started walking toward the door. I put my hand on the
doorknob, turned it, and pulled the door open and stepped out.
I saw two men. I decided if they were looking for me, then, I

was ready to die. I could not take it anymore. What good would I be alive? I decided I would end it all. I ran out and yelled, "Kill me." They look surprised. I told them that they had killed everyone else. I told them that I was a part of the community. I told them that I knew they would come back for me. They ran toward me. I fell on my knees, bracing myself for the bullet that would hit my head or my heart. I knew it would be a matter of minutes.

One man stood over me with the gun. He said I was sure someone else was here. I finally found you. The other man said, "We need this land. We had been trying to get it for years. We decided that the only way to get it was to get rid of the people." He told me that I was in such a secluded area that it would take weeks or even months before someone stopped by. He said they had been watching this community for years. He said they watched people and rode by late at night. He said that they knew everything about this place. They knew where everyone lived and what they did. He told me that they had even attended some of the local people's funeral. People just smiled at us thinking we were relatives of the deceased. I looked up at the men with fear in my eyes and asked them to let me go. They laughed and said no.

They said that they came back for me, and they were going to finish the job. I knew their faces. I had seen them at the local grocery store. They were both dressed in black today, and they were in black before. They kept staring at me and smiling with the gun pointed straight at me. I thought maybe I could run, but I knew I could not escape. The other man said, "You just don't know how long we planned this. We can't let you go. We have to kill you too. We are glad we found you." He put the gun on my forehead. I began to cry. I thought of my parents. I wondered if they were this frightened when they died. I heard the sound of the gun. I felt pain. I felt myself falling.

I heard my name called. I felt someone touching me. I felt something cold on my head. I heard noises. Where was I? The noises got louder. A man was calling me. I heard someone say, "Open your eyes. Please open your eyes." The voice sounded familiar. I had heard this voice before. I heard him say, "I love you. Please, please open your eyes." I opened my eyes and saw my husband. I just looked at him. He asked if I was okay. I asked him what had happened? He said I had a bad dream. He said I was crying, yelling, and screaming, "Don't kill me," over and over again. I felt my forehead. He said that he had placed a wet cloth on my head. He asked me what I was dreaming? He looked at me and said you were sweating.

I sat up in bed. I told Robert about the terrible dream. I asked him for the time. He told me that I was late for work. He said that he left me in bed and waited for my morning call. He said when he did not get it, he got worried. He said he called several times, but there was no answer. He said that he got so worried that he decided to come home and check on me. He was shocked to hear about my dream. I was still shaking as I told him the story. He assured me that it would be okay. He asked if I wanted to take the day off. I smiled and told him no. He said that he would wait for me to dress and he would take me to work. I was glad.

That terrible dream was never discussed again. I still live in that same community. The people still walk by in the morning, smiling and greeting each other. The Johnson kids are still waving. I still go to the small grocery store. Richard is alive, and so is Wanda (the Radford girl). Richard is married with three children; Wanda lives in another state. I am not even sure if they know each other. Ms. Thelma is still sitting on the bench in front of the grocery store fanning flies and bees with her handkerchief. Randy lives in Germany.

I had a terrible dream; it seemed so real. Is it possible that this dream could one day become someone's reality?

Sarah

Sarah grew up in a small town in the south. She was the youngest. Her complexion was darker than her mother's other children. She never knew her father, but she looked a lot like him. Her mother seemed to have cursed the day she was born.

In a big house with her sisters and brothers, Sarah always felt alone. All she had were her dreams, books, and dolls that she rarely played with or touched. Her sisters and brothers constantly teased her. They would call her "mud face," the "ugly duckling," and "no daddy's little child."

Sarah's mother was raped one summer afternoon when she was coming from work. The man who raped her was Sarah's father. Sarah never knew any details. She knew that her mom would call her worthless and would say that she was just like her deadbeat dad. Mr. Johnson, her mother's husband, and the police searched and searched for the man, but were never able to find him.

After months of her mother walking around the house with another man's baby inside of her, Mr. Johnson told her mother that he would keep the baby and raise her as his own. Sarah never knew Mr. Johnson because he died a couple of hours after she was born. Her brothers and sisters accused her of killing their father. They called her a murderer. They often told her that she was the cause of his death and the reason why they did not have a father. They told her that once he saw how ugly she was he had a heart attack. They called her a killer. No matter what they said, Sarah felt he was a nice man too because he allowed her to be in his family.

Rejection, guilt, suicide, and less than a human being were not enough words or phrases to express how Sarah felt. She did everything she could to be accepted and loved by her family.

She would do her sisters' hair, clean their rooms, wash their clothes, run errands, and even lie for them. She did her brothers chores: took out the trash, cleaned the yard, and swept out the old barn house that their father had built in the back to work on his cars. She would even give them the money she had saved up from running errands for some of the old folks in the neighborhood. They would always give her lots of money. Sarah thought they felt sorry for her. Everyone knew how her family treated her. Sometimes the old folks would see her in the yard and give her a dollar or two. They would tell her to put that up for later. They would also tell her to come by and see them if she needed anything.

Sarah was a loner. She so desperately wanted to have friends and a family. She had friends she talked to at school, but they never would come over or invite her to visit them. She loved her mother, and she wanted her to love her. She sometimes felt if she had her mother's love, she would not need anything else. She wanted her to treat her the same way she treated her sisters and brothers. She wanted her to just love her and be proud of her. Sarah was dying inside, and nobody knew except Jabel.

Jabel was her oldest brother. He was twenty-five years old. He was married and lived about seventy-five miles from them. He would visit once a month. During his stay, he would always spend time with her. He and his father had a big argument before she was born, and his father told him to leave and get his own place. He would tell Sarah how much he missed his father and how sorry he was that he disappointed him. She and Jabel could talk about everything. He really loved her, but Sarah knew she could never visit him or stay at his house.

His wife could not have any children, so she appeared to be very jealous of their relationship. As soon as they would start laughing, she would come around and say it was time to go. Jabel and Sarah would just look at each other and smile. Jabel would always give her a hug and tell her that he would see her the next time. Jabel was really nice. He was the only one who showed Sarah any affection.

Jabel knew how she felt about their mother. He would always promise her that things with their mother would get better, and she would treat her differently. Sarah would hold on to that until he would come again. He would always brighten up her day, and he would always give her a gift, toy, or money when he came.

One day, Sarah came home from school and saw her mother crying. She asked what was wrong. Her mother just looked at her and wept even harder. Sarah asked her again, and she told her that her brother Larry had just gotten shot and died instantly.

She said he had been down the street gambling and one of the guys accused him of stealing money. She said the police had arrested the boy that shot him and she was waiting for a ride to go identify the body. I asked if she wanted me to go. She said no. She said the rest of her children would meet her there. Sarah felt so sad for her mother. She loved Larry, too, but she did not want to see her mother in so much pain. She looked at her mother and began to cry too. She reached out to console her mother. She put her arms around her and told her that everything would be okay.

Her mother dried her tears, looked at her, and pushed her away, and told her never to do that again. She told her that God took the wrong child; he should have taken her. Sarah tried to hold back the tears, but she could not. She walked away from her mother then, knowing that they would never have a relationship. She also knew that she would never be a part of the family.

Sarah cried and cried that night. Out of all the things that had happened to her, this was the worst. She tried to call Jabel, but there was no answer. Everyone in the house was quiet, and no one was talking to her. She tried to sleep, but she could not. Every time she closed her eyes, she would hear her mother saying those words over and over again. Sarah was so hurt. She decided that since her mother wanted her dead, she would make it easy. She went into the bathroom, got a razor blade, and cut her wrist until she felt no pain.

Sarah woke up in the city hospital. She looked up, and the nurse was smiling down at her. The nurse asked her how she felt. Sarah told her she felt fine. The nurse told her that she had done a foolish thing. She told her that her mother brought her in and said that she would be back early that morning to see how she was doing. The nurse told her that she had not come, but she would probably be in before noon. Sarah waited and waited, but her mother nor her sisters and brothers showed up. When the nurse came by to check her vital signs, Sarah told her that her mother was probably making funeral arrangements for her brother Larry.

The nurse liked Sarah a lot. She would come in and talk to her. They would laugh, read, and discuss books together and watch television. The nurse had called Sarah's mother a couple of times, but there was no answer. Sarah would ask the nurse about her mother almost every day, but the nurse would tell her that her mother would probably stop by that day. The nurse became very concerned. One day when the social worker came by, the nurse told her about Sarah.

Sarah became more and more depressed thinking about her family. The nurse told her that a social worker would be coming by to see her. Sarah asked why she had to see a social worker. The nurse told her that they had been calling her mother, and her mother asked them to stop calling her. Sarah asked her why and the nurse told her that her mother said that she had no time to deal with a child who wanted to kill herself. The nurse said that her mother told her that the hospital was the best place for suicide patients.

Sarah was so hurt. The social worker came in and talked to her about the options she had to offer Sarah. She told her that she would go to a foster home. She also told her that she had spoken with her mother and her mother said that she was fine with whatever they decided. Before the social worker could finish her conversation with Sarah, the nurse walked in and asked the social worker if Sarah could live with her. Sarah and the social worker were shocked. The social worker looked at Sarah and asked her what she thought. Sarah smiled and told the social worker that she was glad somebody wanted her.

The nurse, Belle, grabbed her and hugged her. She told her that the first day she met her she loved her. She said that she always wanted children but could never have any. She said she and her husband had tried everything. She said they finally gave up after he got sick. She spent all her time taking care of him. She said when he died, she dedicated all her time to just working in the hospital. She said she sometimes felt she was being punished, and she did not know why. She told Sarah that God had answered her prayers and He had not forgotten her. Sarah just smiled. Sarah told her that she had not been praying a lot, but maybe the times that she did, God heard her also.

Belle, the social worker, and Sarah's mother completed all of the important documents. Sarah knew she probably would not see her mother again. She was hurt but felt this was the best decision. She still could not believe that her mother signed the papers so quickly. Arrangements were made for Sarah to stay in the hospital until Belle could take her home. Finally, everything was done, and Sarah was moving to her new home.

Sarah loved her new home, and Belle loved having her there. She immediately enrolled her in the best school. Sarah had the best of everything. She had friends, parties, and weekend and summer trips. She wore the best clothes, and her room was like a page torn from one of the home magazines. She went to New York almost every month to visit Belle's mother.

Sarah even had a grandmother. Belle was an only child. She knew that one day she would have to take care of her mother. Her health was not as good as it once was. She had told Sarah that they would probably move to New York one day. Sarah knew she would miss her new friends, but she was willing to go anywhere with Belle.

The day finally came. One day when Sarah got home from high school, Belle told her they had to leave. She told her that she had already called her school and transferring would not be a problem. She told Sarah to call her friends and tell them that she would be leaving in the morning. Sarah was sad that night. She laid in bed thinking about the big change she would have to make, but most of all, about her mother and her sisters and brothers she would have to leave behind. She had not seen or heard from them since she had been with Belle, but Belle had seen her mother in the store. Belle said she walked up to her and told her how well I was doing. She said that she also gave her my picture. She said my mother smiled and said thank you. Sarah wanted to call her mother. She asked Belle what she thought. Belle told her to call. Sarah called, but the number had been changed. She thought about calling Jabel, but she did not.

The house in New York was bigger than the one they left in the South. Belle had gotten a realtor to sell the property. Sarah had been in the house numerous times, but it seemed as if it had gotten larger. Belle never discussed her financial business with Sarah. Belle was so nice to her. She treated her like a real mother would treat her daughter. She was also nice to her mother. She made sure she got the best care in the nursing home. Belle would visit her almost every day. Sarah would visit on weekends. They did this for years until Grandma Ruby died.

Belle was sad, but she would always tell Sarah that she had no regrets. She would tell her that her mother was in a better place. Sarah loved Grandma Ruby. She treated her so nicely. She treated her like she was really her granddaughter. Grandma Ruby would call her "my baby." Sarah did not think people could love you like this until she met Belle and Grandma Ruby. Sarah always would talk to Belle about Grandma Ruby's funeral. She would ask Belle why everyone was so happy. Belle would just smile and tell her that her mom was enjoying the journey.

Belle was so good to Sarah. She told Sarah that she would support her all the way and she did. She was there for her prom, her first date, her three attempts at trying to get her driving licenses, her graduations, her school dances, parties, etc. She had the best doctors, joined the best organizations and sorority, and had the best therapists. Belle insisted that Sarah see a therapist. She was in therapy for two years.

Sarah loved Belle and Belle loved Sarah. Belle made sure that Sarah attended the best schools, college, and medical school. Belle was so excited the day Sarah received her BS degree in Biology. She could not get through the crowd quick enough. She was making her way to Sarah when she heard her yell out, "Mom, I am over here." Belle cried and when she finally got to her, she embraced Sarah so tightly. She told her that she could not ask for a better daughter. Belle and Sarah grew closer and closer. Belle was there for all of her accomplishments, honors, and graduation from medical school. Belle and Sarah talked about everything. They would talk about Sarah's plans and her family. Sarah would always tell her that no matter what attempts she had made in trying to contact them, they were all unsuccessful.

After four years of being a medical doctor, Sarah decided she wanted to take Belle to Europe. Belle and Sarah were so excited. All Belle talked about was the trip. Belle and her best friend, Ms. Carolyn, were out shopping when Belle fainted. By the time Sarah got the telephone call and got to the hospital, Belle had died.

Sarah's heart was broken. Everyone was there for her. Belle had left all of her directions about the arrangements with her lawyer. Belle left her everything. It was so strange for Sarah. She did not know how she would manage. Belle had left her a note. She told her everything to do and told her not to be sad because she was enjoying the journey.

Sarah wiped away her tears and smiled to herself. She pulled herself together and took care of all the arrangements, just like her mother had requested. Ms. Carolyn was there for her, and so were her friends.

After the funeral, Sarah decided to make a visit to the south. She had not been there for more than twenty years. Things had changed. She stopped by to see Ms. Simms, the social worker. She had kept in touch with her and Belle. Ms. Simms was saddened by Belle's death, but she told Sarah that she knew she would be okay. Sarah asked Ms. Simms about her biological mother.

She said that she had not seen her, but she knew that she was sick. Sarah told her that she was going by to see her. Ms. Simms told her that she thought that was a good idea. She told her that she thought most of her sisters and brothers had left the area and that her mother was living by herself.

Sarah arrived at the house. She knocked on the door, and this grey-haired woman answered the door. Sarah knew it was her mother. The lady asked if she needed help. Sarah asked her if she recognized her. The lady said, "No, I have never seen you before, honey." Sarah asked her if she could come in. The lady was polite and invited her into the house. Sarah looked around. It seemed that everything was the same. Nothing had changed. The same marks were on the wall and it seemed as if the same curtains were at the window. The lady asked Sarah if she could help her. She asked her about her children. She told her that her oldest son, Jabel, and his wife had moved to Florida. Martha and Laura moved to Connecticut with their father's family. Gary died three months after his twin Larry. She said that Gary was trying to hurt the boys that shot his brother and they shot him. She said Carol left home one night with some man and never returned. She said that Melvin and Thomas were both in prison for rape. Sarah then asked her about her youngest daughter.

She said Sarah left. I gave her up to foster care. She left with a nurse at the hospital. I have not seen her for a while now. I am sure she is doing well. I never treated her right. I hated her for what someone else did to me. A man raped me one afternoon, and the police never found him. I guess he is dead by now, the lady said, but I had a good husband. He wanted me to keep the baby. He wanted to raise her as his own. The lady said she just did not know how to be a mother. The pain that man caused made me give up something precious that was meant for me. I remembered his face and the older she got, the more she looked like him. That child loved me and would do anything for me. I signed those papers, because every time I saw her I felt the pain and hurt. I hated her for something someone had done to me. I truly gave up something precious. I am sure that if Sarah was around, she would be here loving and caring for me. When I recognized what I had done, it was too late. I am sure she had a great life, and she deserved every bit of it. As she talked, tears rolled down Sarah's eyes. The lady said, "I don't have much time to live; I am very sick. I have called my children, but none of them have come to help me." She said she had decided that she would probably die alone.

Sarah looked at the lady and told her that no one should die alone. She told her that she would be in town for a while, and if she didn't mind, she would come by and visit and make sure she would get the best doctor and health care. She said, "I have money, transportation, and a facility for you to go to; these people will take good care of you."

The lady asked her who she was. She asked her where she came from. She asked why she was so nice to her. She wanted to know why she was so interested in her life and the life of her children. She asked, "Are you an angel?" Sarah told her that she was the youngest daughter. She told her that she was the one that she left in the hospital. She told her that she was the one that she gave to the nurse. Sarah told her that she had never forgotten her. She told her that not a day goes by that she does not think of her. She told her that even though she was given the best of everything, she would love to have been near her and her sisters and brothers. The lady started to weep. She asked Sarah to forgive her. She told her that she was sorry that she had not been a better mother.

Sarah moved her mother to New York and took good care of her until she died. She gave her the best that money could buy. She had the best doctors and she was given the best care.

Sarah

Every now and then she would get a call from one of her siblings asking about their mother. Jabel called often. None of them believed that she would do this for her mother after how badly all of them treated her. They too thanked her for being there since none of them were able to assist. Before her mother died, she told Sarah that she was proud of her and that she loved her. Her mother died in her arms. As Sarah closed her mother's eyes, she told her to enjoy the journey.

Sarah took care of all of the funeral arrangements. Her mother was buried beside her stepfather.

The Day The Earth Shook

It was five o'clock in the morning. The rain was beating heavily on the window sill. The thunder was roaring, and the lightning was flashing almost nosily. It lit up my entire room. I laid in the bed restless as I wondered what the day would bring. Michael was out visiting the sick, and I had an appointment to meet the new musician at two. I had to get up and start my day. All of a sudden, my mind took me back to that incident. I thought about the fear I felt and the pain I saw in her eyes. I wondered if I could have done anything to prevent that awful ordeal. It had been some years now, but every now and then the thoughts would come to my mind, and I would think about her and how my life had changed for the better.

Lillian was a very attractive teenager. She had beautiful brown skin. Her skin looked as if it were covered with brown velvet fabric that enveloped not only her face but her entire body. She had a special glow that attracted all men. She was about 5'7," 125 pounds, and she had a figure that looked as if it was formed by an artist. She was always well dressed and had that "I just left the hair salon" hairdo and everything else just fell in place. She was well-liked and admired by all.

The Day The Earth Shook

We had decided to go to the corner store after school. Yes, just like all kids we had been told over and over by our parents not to go, but who listened to parents. We were at that age when parents did not know as much as we did. They were old-fashioned and had no idea what good times were. Things had changed since the forties.

At sixteen years old, we were trying to be adults and do what adults did, so wanted to see how it felt to smoke and drink. We stopped by Mr. Raleigh's store to pick up the items. We told him that we were getting everything for our parents. We picked up chips too, so that he would think everything was okay and on the up and up. He knew children could not come to the store without buying something for themselves. Although the lie was working, it just seemed wrong to deceive him, but that was the way it was. The whole day seemed wrong. I am not sure what it was, but it did not feel like a regular day. It seemed as if something bad was going to happen. It seemed dreary, damp, and eerie.

On the way out of the store, I noticed an old man smiling at us. That was not unusual because everywhere Lillian went someone was smiling, whistling, looking or just telling her how beautiful she was. He called out to us ask us if he could give us some money or if he could take us to the movies. We ignored him and continued walking. We were only interested in what we had in the bags and how quickly we were going to use everything.

After walking for almost a block, we stopped by Michael's house. That was the hangout. Michael's parents were never home. It seemed like Michael was in charge. He cooked for them. Michael was a good guy. He liked us and treated us like sisters. He would tell us what not to do, who not to talk to, where not to go. We never listened, but we knew Michael was concerned about our safety. Michael asked us what we had in the bag. He looked in, shook his head, and started eating our chips. It didn't take us but a minute before Michael started fussing about what was in the bags and how we should not be tampering with things we were not able to handle.

Michael's father was a minister, and that was his dream also. He had already preached enough sermons to us for him to be ordained. When he was not telling us about the Lord and why we should read the Bible, he also spent time telling us what young ladies should and should not do. Michael was nineteen and acted as if he was twenty-five with children, a wife, and a job. We tolerated him though, not only was he concerned about our souls, but us individually. He would always tell us how he wanted the best for us and how he would pray for us daily. He would tell us that one day we would make some man happy. We would both look at him and roll our eyes.

We left Michael's house feeling guilty about the stuff in the bag. We decided that we would give the bag to the first person we saw. We talked a little about what Michael had said, but immediately we started talking about our plans for the next day. It was summer time, school was out, and we had the whole summer to enjoy life.

My house was the first house we came to, so I said goodnight and walked in the gate. I still had the bag, so I put it beside the mailbox and ran in. Lillian lived five houses down. Usually, I would walk her halfway, but the bathroom was calling. I ran to the bathroom, and while in there, I realized that she had my ring. When I finished, I ran after her.

As I got closer to her house, I saw her talking to a man in a car. I thought it was Mr. Ron who lived down the street, so I call out to both of them. The car door opened and Lillian got in. They sped by me. I knew then it was the man at the store. I did not hear from Lillian anymore that night. I did not want to call the house just in case this was some kind of plan Lillian and this man had come up with. Lillian had done this before. One time I called the house looking for her, but she had gone out with her friend. Lillian got in big trouble. She told her Mom that she was at my house. When her Mom started asking me questions, I did not know what to say. I got in trouble too. We were both punished for two weeks. We could not come out of the house for anything.

I could not sleep at all. I talked to Michael all night. I told him that as soon as I saw daylight, I would go out looking for her. I told him that I was worried about her. He told me that she was probably okay. I told him that I was going to find her in the morning. He told me not to go out without an adult. He told me to come get him in the morning.

Morning could not come quick enough. I got up, put my clothes on, slipped out of the house, and picked up my grandfather's walking stick. I also had an extra bag of clothes with me just in case Lillian had told the same lie; this way she would go home dressed in a different outfit. I started walking, and all of a sudden, it seemed as if I heard a scream. I continued to run, and I started calling Lillian's name. I did not hear anything. I just kept running. In the distant, I thought I heard a cry. I followed the path through the woods where we would have cookouts in the summer. I saw what looked like an animal. I got frightened because daddy told me about a fox that would come out at night. I thought it was the fox. All I had was that stick and I was going to use that. I started screaming, thinking he would move, but the closer I got, the less it moved. I kept running. When I was right on top of the animal, I realized it was Lillian.

Lillian was lying there. Her clothes were torn and almost off. She was crying. I knelt down beside her and prayed for strength for me to help get her up. Tears were rolling down her face. She put her hands to her face and her knuckles were bloody. I just sat beside her and cried. I took my jacket off and tried to hide parts of her naked body. I did not know what to do. I told her I was sorry. She grabbed my hand and held it so tightly. I told her that I had to go get help. She told me not to leave. I asked her who had done this and she told me about the man we saw in the store. I told her that we needed to go get help. She told me no. I could not believe Lillian was saying that. She said that her mother and father would be angry with her and that she would probably lose all of her friends. I asked her what friends she was talking about. I told her that Michael and I would not stop caring for her. I told her we were friends until the end. I told her that was a silly thing to say, People in our town cared. They would do all they could do to stop this man. She said no and pushed me away from her. I looked at her, not knowing what to say, do, or think. She pushed me again and started reaching for her clothes. She told me that she knew the man and had been out with him before. She said this time everything went wrong. She told me she was in some pain, but she wanted to go home. I told her that I would walk with her. I asked her if she was sure she did not want to go to the doctor. She said that she wanted me to promise her that I would not tell anyone. She said not only that, but she wanted me to forget it happened and that I found her like this. She said she had it all worked out; it would never happen to her again. I begged her to let me walk her home. In a cruel voice, she said, " I told you no." She told me that our friendship was over. She told me that I deserved a better friend, and she wanted me to find a respectable friend. She said she wanted me to find someone who cares more about themselves. I apologized for not helping her and told her that this situation could only bring us closer. She said that I meant nothing to her anymore. I cried. She looked at me and said goodbye. She got up enough strength to get up. She told me that she would make it home okay. She told me that I could leave. She said she would get home okay.

I stood by the tree and looked at her. I knew that this was only temporary. I did not know what she had been through, but surely, it had affected her more than I could ever imagine. I knew our friendship was not over.

Lillian got her clothes, picked up her gym bag, and left the area. I stood there feeling as if my body had been torn into small pieces. We had been friends for a long time. I had lost my best friend, or she was trying to make me feel that way.

I went home and called Lillian several times, but no one answered the telephone. That same night Lillian committed suicide. I had heard of people doing that, but no one in my neighborhood. I had only had seen people talk about that on television. No one ever talked about what happened. We only heard that her Mom found her in a pool of blood. Her Mom was hospitalized for three weeks after Lillian's funeral.

Two weeks after her death, they found the man. I could not keep that secret. I told everything. He was sentenced to life without parole. Lillian was not the only girl he had hurt. She was number six. People drove miles to get to that courthouse to sit in that trial. Lillian's mom was not physically able to attend. My mom did not want me to go, but my Dad said it was necessary.

The man did not seem to care what happened to him. He said some inappropriate things about the girls. He also blamed the girls for what he did to them. He said they wanted everything that happened. Everyone in court looked shocked after he spoke.

Tears rolled down my eyes every time I thought of her. I never found another friend like Lillian. I thought about her whenever there were big events such as the prom, graduation, football games, my first day of college, meeting my boyfriend, and other things. I often wondered what Lillian would have become if she would have lived. I missed her. Life had taken so many twists and turns, but her memory was always present.

The telephone rang. I looked at the clock. I had really spent a lot of time that day thinking about Lillian. I picked up the telephone knowing that the person on the other end would give me some bad news, but it was Michael. We talked about our plans for the afternoon. After I got off the telephone with Michael, I thought about how we ended up together.

After Lillian's death, everything changed. I did not hang out as much. After school, I went home. Everyone was a little frightened after what happened to Lillian. After graduation, I went to college, and Michael moved to another state. He would call sometimes. A year after Michael moved, his parents died. It seemed as if they died right behind each other. His mom had a stroke and died. About three months later, his father died of pneumonia. I did not attend either funeral. Both were large because they knew everybody in town and the neighboring cities.

I was at home thinking about plans for my life when the telephone rang. I wondered who would be calling. I took my time answering the telephone. I was shocked to hear the voice on the other end; it was Michael. He sounded the same. Years had really gone by. I was glad to hear his voice. He said he was in town and he was coming by to see me. I told him that I was still at the house. My parents had moved into my grandmother's house in the country, and they left me with their house. I told him I would be waiting to see him. He laughed and called me a homeowner and said he would be by shortly.

I jumped out of bed, showered, and dressed quickly. I pulled out all of my old albums because I knew we were going to spend at least two hours talking and laughing about people. Waiting patiently for Michael, I thought about how he must look now. He was handsome. He was always exercising and eating healthy. He was like a brother to us. I guess every time I looked at him, I saw him that way. I was sure he had grown up now and gotten more good looking. I wondered if he had a female friend, and, if not, if there was hope for us in the future. Feeling embarrassed by the thought, I thought of Carl. Carl was my boyfriend. Carl was in the hospital and was expected to be out soon. What was I thinking? Michael was a friend. He would always have a special place in my heart. The doorbell rang. It was Michael.

Michael looked more handsome than ever. He looked as if he had gotten taller. I looked up at him and I am sure my heart stopped beating for about a couple of seconds. I felt like I could not breathe for a minute. He looked at me, smiled, grabbed me, and kissed me on my cheek. He asked me if I was going to invite him in. I laughed and said, "Come on in and have a seat." He grabbed me by my arm and embraced me. His big body almost smothered me. He looked down at me and told me that he missed me and that he still misses Lillian. He said no matter what he does in life, the memory of her death would never leave him. Tears rolled down my cheeks as he talked. He wiped my cheeks with his handkerchief. He grabbed me again and told me how happy he was to see me. The smell of his cologne almost hypnotized me. He smelled so good. I thanked him for wiping my tears and asked him if he wanted some tea.

I gave Michael the tea, and his eyes just seemed to follow me. I asked him if he was okay and he said that he really missed me. He said he thought about me often but was afraid to call me. He said that he did not want to get in the way of my success nor all of my male suitors. I just laughed. He said that he had been reading about me. He said that although he had moved away, he was still getting copies of the local paper. Gaston would mail him one every week. (Gaston was the owner of the paper company.) He said not only was he reading about me, but he was also seeing those beautiful pictures of me. I smiled. He said it seemed as if I was doing one great thing after another. He asked me who was the guy who was always in the pictures with me. He asked me if that was my escort or my fiancé. I told him that was my boyfriend. I told him that Carl was in the hospital and no marriage plans had been made. He asked me how long we had been dating. I told him seven years. He looked at me and said, "Well, maybe we still have a chance." I did not respond. I asked him to tell me more about his job. He said that could wait. He asked me if I had plans for the evening. Forgetting that I had made plans to see Carl and his mother, I said no. He said he wanted to take me out to dinner. I said okay. He handed me his cup and said he would pick me up around seven. He said he had to take care of some business first. He kissed me on my cheek and said he would see me later. I unlocked the door for him. As he was walking towards the gate, I got a back view of him, and I liked what I saw.

I could not wait for that dinner. I spent most of the afternoon looking for that special dress and special shoes to wear. I also spent some of the day talking to Carl and his mother. I told both of them that I would not be at the hospital because something came up. They both understood. Thank God Carl was doing better.

Michael was on time. At seven, the doorbell rang. I ran to the door, and he stood there with a dozen roses. My mouth opened. He gave them to me and gave me a kiss on the cheek. I put the roses on the table. He followed me. I looked back and saw he was dressed in a black suit. He looked better than he did hours ago. He told me that I looked beautiful and that he would be honored to be in my company for the evening. I smiled. I locked the door. He held my hand and escorted me to his car. He opened the door for me. Michael was always a gentleman. Not comparing the two, but Carl never saw the need to be a gentleman. He was all for women's liberation. As I sat in the car and listened to Michael talk about the changes in the town, I noticed the gray hair in his beard and the gray hair in his mustache that covered his upper lip so perfectly. His thick eyebrows looked as if an artist had painted them on his face, and his perfect hairline outlined his brown muscular face so well. He grabbed my hand as he was driving and asked me if I was listening to him. I told him yes. He asked me about my mother. I told him that she was fine, and so was my father. He told me that he would love to see both of them. As he talked, I asked myself if it was possible for us to be a couple. I admired him, and I had always liked him. In a strong voice, Michael said, "We are here." He jumped out of the car, opened the door, and we walked into the restaurant.

We were seated at the best table. He smiled at me and said that he had been waiting for the question, but since I had not asked it, he would tell me. He said his dream came true. He told me that he was a minister. I looked at him and told him that I was sure he was a great minister. He said that since his father was, he was almost sure that he was going to follow in his footsteps. He said that God had blessed him with everything. He talked about the church. He talked about his members and his sermons. I looked at him with such joy. Again, Michael said that God had blessed him with everything except a wife. I looked at him, not knowing what to say. He said that he always had this special girl in mind, but he was not sure if she felt the same way about him. I told him that any woman would be glad to have him as a husband and father for her children. He asked me if I felt the same way. I said yes. At that moment, the waiter came to the table; he asked us what we wanted to drink. I ordered tea. I told Michael that I needed to check on Carl. He said okay. I called the hospital, and Carl's sister answered the telephone. I asked her how Carl was doing. She said that Carl had gotten worse. He had to have surgery. I dropped the telephone, and told Michael I needed to go. He left some money on the table and said he was right behind me. We got in the car, and he asked what happened. I told him I did not know. There was silence in the car. Michael put on some gospel music to comfort me. I appreciated it, but I could not focus on anything at the time. Michael dropped me off at the entrance and I ran to the desk.

I asked about Carl. The nurse told me that the family was in the waiting area on the fourth floor. The elevator was so slow, I got off and took the stairs. When I got to the fourth floor, I saw Carl's mom and his sister. They had tears in their eyes. I asked them if Carl was okay. His sister told me that Carl died five minutes ago. I almost fainted. Michael caught me. She said that Carl had bled internally and the doctors could not stop the bleeding. Carl was born with a rare disease, and every once in a while, he would get sick and be hospitalized. His mother felt that he would get better, but Carl had gotten worse. He would not talk much about his illness. He would just say that he was afraid that one day he would not leave the hospital. I would tell him not to worry because that would not happen, but Carl's words had come true. I was so hurt. I cried in his mother's arms. His sister asked me who was the young man with me. I told her he was a minister. His mom and sister thanked him for being there for the family. They thought he was the chaplin in the hospital.

Carl's mom told me that it was okay. She said she felt Carl was resting and no longer in pain. She said that he would be cremated. She told me that she wanted me to a part of everything. She said that even though we never married, she saw me as her daughter-in-law. Michael excused himself. They thanked him again. Michael told me that he would give me a call later. They looked at him and me and just thanked him again.

Michael called around midnight. He said he was coming over. I said okay. As soon as he entered the house, I just cried and cried. He told me that it would be okay and that he would be by my side as long as I needed him. He held me in his arms. After realizing that I was in his arms, I pulled away. I could not believe that I was allowing this man to hold me when Carl had not been dead for eight hours. Michael pulled me back and kissed me. He looked at me and said, "Let's go get some dessert." He told me that things could not be helped, but just being near me was something he would always cherish.

It was a nice summer night, and the ice cream was really good. Our town had really changed. We now had stores and restaurants that stayed open past nine o'clock. I was having a great time, but I could not stop thinking about Carl.

I looked at Michael. He looked at me. I told him that this was not right. He asked me if he had done something wrong. I told him I had. He asked what had happened. I told him that

Carl had died and I was out with another man and enjoying every moment. I told him I had only kissed Carl for the last seven years. In those years, I never felt like I was feeling with him. He looked at me and said that Carl had been in love with me for several years, but he had been in love with me all his life. He said from the day he met me, he wanted me to be his wife. I looked at him and said I am younger than you. He said it did not matter. He always liked me. He asked me if I knew why he really came back. I told him that I did not know. He said that he always loved me, but never told me because I was always asking him about other guys. He said that after Lillian's death, he felt our friendship was over, so he stopped calling and writing. He said that I did not answer his telephone calls. He said that he thought that I blamed myself for Lillian's death, but I would never talk to him about it. He also said that when his parents died, someone told him that I was almost married. They told him that I was engaged to a boy named Carl. He said that was it. He decided that he would not call. He said that he felt he had to move on. He did, but he could not get me off his mind. He said that after fighting what he felt, he gave in and decided that regardless of what my life would be, he had to come back and try one more time. He held my hand and told me that he really loved me and asked me to marry him. I looked puzzled but knew Michael meant every word he had just said. I smiled, kissed him on his cheek, and asked him to take me home.

He walked in the door, grabbed me, and kissed me good night. I told him good night. I watched him as he walked to the car. I was so confused. I wanted to call my mother, but I knew she was asleep, and the telephone call would startle her and she would not get back to sleep. I thought about Michael. It seemed as if the earth was shaking inside my heart. I felt like there had been a terrible storm and everything had been thrown all over the place and re-arranged. I laid in bed thinking and crying. I did not know what to do. I wanted to talk to my mom. She always had the right answers. I felt like there had been a terrible storm. How could I be so sad and so happy at the same time? I had just lost my boyfriend.

Carl was good in his own way. I knew he loved me; so did his family. His dad was never around. He used to be the neighborhood drunk. Carl vowed that he would never be like him. Carl started taking care of his family at an early age. His father never did and left town with Ms. Johnnie and her three children. We never found out for sure, but rumor had it that the one inside Ms. Johnnie's stomach belonged to Carl's father. We do know that the three that she had had different fathers. Carl's dad was the talk of the town. On any given day when he was living in town, you could see him staggering down the street with a bottle in his hand, cursing, and telling everyone that would listen that his wife was so mean to him. He would tell people that she put him out of his own house. That really was not true.

Carl's mother lived in her mother's house. Carl often told the story of how he would hear his mom beg his father to put them in a better house. He said his father would say, "Nothing is wrong with this one; we are going to stay in this one until it rots." Carl saw his mom do all of the work. She worked from sun up to sun down to make things comfortable for her children. It was not until her father died and she got all of his insurance money that she stopped working. We never knew how much she got, but it was a matter of days that she sold that house and moved uptown in a nice house. She stopped working, brought herself a new car, and started doing volunteer work. Carl and his family were the talk of the town for a couple of months.

Ms. Johnnie came back to town. To this day, no one knows what happened to Carl's father. She called his mom and said he was dead and that she was sorry for any pain she caused. She also said she would not be at the funeral. Ms. Johnnie started going to church and got a job in the post office. After the girls finished high school, one by one they went to New York with her aunt. Ms. Johnnie finally moved to New York with them.

Everyone just stopped talking about Carl's father. Carl would just say, "I am going to show people that I am different than my father." He did that. Carl was highly respected. He was an educator. He was a professor at the college and the president of the local school board. He had hoped to become a superintendent. A lot of people knew him, and they knew about his illness. I think Carl didn't propose because he did not know how long he had on earth.

I woke up around six o'clock in the morning. I thought about Michael. I smiled because I thought I had had a terrible nightmare. As I went over the incidents in my mind, I realized I was not dreaming. I sat up quickly on one side of the bed and wondered what I would do.

I called mom. She was still resting. I told her the news. She was silent for about ten seconds, and then she asked me how I felt. I told her words could not express how I was feeling. She asked me how Carl's mother was. I told her I had not talked to her since I left the hospital. She asked me about getting the train since she felt it was too much for daddy to drive. I told her not to worry, because Carl was going to be cremated. She said that she would call Carl's mom and talk to her. I told her that I was sure she wanted to hear her voice. Mom and Ms. Lima were friends in high school. They were happy about Carl and me being a couple, but neither interfered in our relationship. Every now and then Ms. Lima would tell me that Carl really loved me. I would look and respond the way I had been taught. I would say, "I love him too, Ms. Lima."

Carl was on my mind. Michael had brought a lot of confusion, but I had to deal with Carl's death. Carl and I had some fun times together. I knew the relationship had to come to an end eventually because I never felt the same way he felt about me. I knew I was going to have to confront him, but I never thought death would be the dividing point. Wow! It was so upsetting. I felt so bad about all of this. Carl would have probably been a good husband, but I could never have been a good wife to him. I had mentioned my feelings to my mom one time, and she said, "Just go with it, honey. It doesn't always have to be equal, just endure, and it will get better." She said I endured, and things are much better for me. I never told mom anything else about how I felt about Carl, nor did I ask her if she felt that way about my Dad.

I was sure his sister and mother were making all of the arrangements. I would have to go. I would have to show my face. I knew they wanted to ask my opinion. Carl's mom saw me as the daughter-in-law anyway. It was two days before the memorial service. I had to make it, and I had to be strong for his mom. The one thing that Carl would want would be for me to be there for his mom.

The telephone rang. I knew it was Michael. I was prepared to tell him that he had to give me some space until everything was over. I said hello. It was Carl's mother. I asked her if she was okay. She said she was doing the best she could since she had lost her oldest child and her son. She asked me how I was doing. I told her that I was trying to adjust, and that was all I could do. She told me that her prayers were with me and that she was having a hard time accepting what had happened. She said, "I was waiting for his phone call this morning." Carl would call his mom every morning around seven. She said seven-thirty came and she wondered why Carl had not called. She said then she remembered he would not be calling anymore. We both cried.

I felt so foolish. Carl was dead. I was sitting at his memorial service thinking about what Michael had said. He talked to me all the way to the service. He told me he would not call but would wait until I was ready to give him a call. He said he knew I needed to have some time. He said he would be in town and not leave until he heard from me.

The service was very upbeat. Carl's mom had the best of everything. The university choir sang, and everyone said great things about Carl. There were times when I thought, "Who are they talking about." Everyone kept watching me. I guess they were expecting me to have an outburst; maybe they thought someone was supposed to fan me until I fainted and someone took me out, but I did fine. I cried. I was sad. It felt as if my heart was turning inside of my body. All I could think about was if I felt like this what was Carl's mother feeling. I pained for her also. After the service, Carl's sister came to me and told me that I was all Carl talked about. She said that for some reason, he felt he was not good enough. She said he often talked about when he was able to give me what I deserved he was going to propose. I looked at her, and she looked at me. She said that she missed her brother, but she knew my heart was bleeding also. As she said that a burst of cold air ran up and down my body. She embraced me and said, "We will always be family. I know in time, you will find the man that will make you happy, but you will always be my sister-in-law." We hugged again. She told me that she was moving back into the house with her mom, and she wanted me to come by and visit. I promised her I would.

My heart was not only bleeding, but it was also torn into pieces. I was a hurt and lonely girlfriend with my mind steadily thinking about another man. Everyone consoled me. I kind of felt the same pain when Lillian died. It was a pain of hopelessness. I could not do anything about Lillian's death, and I could not do anything about Carl's death. Two good people who had influenced my life in one way or another had moved on. We were there consoling his mom and eating all the food that the people had brought by. It looked as if Carl's mom had aged 10 years. I told her that I had to go home. She said she understood. She said she knew I was exhausted. I told her that I would try to get some sleep. I went home, kicked my shoes off, and jumped in the bed.

There was a knock on the door. I sat up, not knowing where I was. My memory finally came back, and I jumped up and ran to the door. It was Michael. I invited him in. He asked me if I were okay. I looked at him and before I could make a sound, he kissed me. We kissed and kissed. He pushed me away and told me how sorry he was that I had to experience so much pain alone. He held me closed and told me how much he loved me. He told me that he knew this was not a good time, but selfishness had overpowered him. He asked me how much time I needed to get over Carl, and when would I be ready to marry him. I laughed but realized very quickly that he was serious. I looked at him and told him that everything was happening too fast. I told him that I liked Carl a lot and that Carl had been there for me the last seven years. I told him that Carl was the man in my life and that I had been faithful to him. He looked at me and said, "I know you are that kind of woman. These are the things I admired about you." He said so you did not answer my questions. I looked at him and said, "I am ready to marry you today." He began telling me about his church and his congregation. He told me that I would make a perfect first lady; he said that God had answered his prayers. He said he needed a wife and he had finally gotten one. He quoted a verse from the Bible. He said, "Proverbs 18:22 says, *"He who finds a wife finds a good thing, and obtains favor from the Lord."*" I just looked at him. He told me that he would be the best husband and I would never want for anything. He told me that he would love me forever. He told me that he had to go back to Dallas and would return in one month. He said his plane left in an hour. I looked at him and asked him what was happening. He smiled and said that he was getting ready to marry the woman that he loves. He kissed me, said goodbye, and said he had to catch a flight. He said that he would return in one month. He said he had to prepare for his new bride.

I sat in the middle of the bed, shocked, confused, and happy. I did not know where to turn, what to do, who to call. All I knew was I like what I was hearing, but Carl had just died; I had gotten a promotion on my job; I was liking being close to my parents, and Michael wanted me to move to Dallas. I was going to be Michael's wife, and I was happy about it. I sat quietly and began to talk to God. I asked God if Michael was the right man for me. I asked God if I was making a mistake. I asked God if this was what He wanted me to do. I can't say I got an audible answer, but I felt calm; I felt happy; I felt at peace; I felt that was my answer. I fell asleep.

Hours had passed by. I woke up happy and called my mother and told her everything. I did not wait for her to say anything. All of a sudden, I heard her crying. I asked what was wrong. I told her I would be okay. I told her that we would come and see them and they could come to visit us and stay as long as they wanted to. She asked me when did Michael leave. I looked at the clock and said he should be there by now. I wondered why he has not called. There was silence on the telephone. I asked my mother if she was okay. She asked me if I had heard the news. I asked her what news. She asked if I saw the special report or the news flash. I asked her what she was talking about. She told me that there was a special report on television that the one o'clock flight going to Dallas crashed, and there were no survivors. She said that it was on television now. I could not move; I dropped the telephone. I heard mom calling me, but I could not answer. I felt the same way that I felt when I heard that Lillian had committed suicide. I opened my mouth, but there was no sound. All I could hear was my mother calling my name. Tears poured down my face. I could not believe that I was going through this again. How much could I bear? Was I supposed to be happy? Was I supposed to have anyone in my life? What had I done wrong? Maybe I was the cause of Lillian dying; maybe I could have helped. Maybe I was getting punished for her death. Maybe I should have been honest with Carl. I should not have made him believe I loved him. Why was everything in my life crumbling? Why was everything I cared about taken away? Why did everyone I knew or cared for commit suicide, had an incurable disease, and now a plane crash? What was wrong? What was wrong with me? I screamed. I called for my mother and God to help me. My mother was trying to comfort me on the phone. Through my tears, I told her that Michael had made me happy. I heard my mom sobbing on the telephone. I put the phone on the receiver. The phone rang and rang, but I refused to talk to anyone, and I refused to watch television. I wanted to remember Michael the way I saw him, and not see him as one of the bodies they were removing from the plane.

I cried. I knew God was not punishing me. He was not that kind of God. I knew He loved me. I felt as if all the blood had been drained from my body. I was in pain. My body was throbbing. Never in my life had I experienced what I felt. No one could have prepared me for this. I believed I was dying. I felt numb. I was ready to die. I had never thought about leaving this world, but it seemed as if I had nothing to live for. I was devastated; I was losing it. I had to get myself together. I had to shake that thought. I knew no matter what happened, God gave me a life, and I had to fulfill His will.

There was a knock on the door. I did not want to see anybody. I did not want anyone to tell me anything. I just wanted to be left alone. The person continued to knock, and the knock got louder and louder. I finally got up and yelled, "What do you want?" They continued to knock. I pulled the door open, and Michael grabbed me. I pushed him away and asked him if he was alright. He said yes. He said he missed his flight and he decided that he was not leaving without me. He said he was in town talking to some old friends. He was getting ready to ask me if I remembered some person when I interrupted him and asked him about the plane crash. He asked, "What plane crash?" I pulled him in and turned on the television. He told me that he had not heard about the crash. We both prayed for the victims and thanked God that he was safe. I held on to Michael. I would not let him go. I called my mom and told her the good news. She talked to Michael also. Even dad talked to him. She asked me if I was sure I wanted to do this thing and if Michael was a replacement for Carl. I told her I was sure. She said she was happy for me and told us to tell her everything.

Michael smiled at me and said he was so happy that I had agreed to be his wife. He told me that he had the perfect plan. He said that we would drive down to my parent's house and get married there. I told him okay. He said that he had some last-minute shopping to do and he would be back. I told him that I would get dressed and be ready by the time he got back. He said he knew a couple of ministers there and he would see if one of them would do the wedding.

Thirty minutes passed, and I called mom back. Dad answered the telephone. That was strange because he did not like talking on the telephone. I asked to speak to mom and he said that they were waiting for the paramedics. I asked what happened. He said that all of a sudden mom had problems breathing. He called her doctor, and he told him to get her to the hospital. I was sick again. I got off the phone, called Michael, and told him the news. Michael said he was on his way, and we would go right there.

I ran around the house as quickly as possible. I had just purchased a new dress so I decided that I would get married in that. I called my hair stylist, explained the situation, and she told me to come right in. I called Michael back, and he told me that he would meet me there. I called my dad and told him that we were on our way.

It was three o'clock when we walked into the room. The doctor, my dad, and the chaplain were there. I walked over to the bed. Mom smiled, pulled down her oxygen apparatus, and said, "I would not miss this for the world." I asked her what was wrong. She told the chaplain to get started.

Michael walked in and said, "Your dad told me to get dressed because your mom wanted us to have the ceremony in her room." I looked at Michael and remembered him telling me to wear my dress and he was going to wear his suit. He wiped the tear that was rolling down my cheek and told me everything would be okay. I asked him about his minister. He told me it was okay.

The ceremony was short and sweet. The rings were beautiful. Michael had picked both of them out. I was so happy but sad to see mom looking as if it was taking everything out of her to breathe. I asked the doctor if she was okay. He told me that she had had this problem for some time but did not want him to tell me. She said that my father was aware, and he had been making sure she was taking care of herself. I looked at mom. She grabbed my hand and said that my happiness was all she needed to see. Mom closed her eyes, and tears rolled down her face. She wiped her face and said it will be fine. She said that God had answered her prayers. She said that Michael was a good man and she knew he was the right one for me. I asked the doctor if she was in a lot of pain. He said no. Mom called Michael and Dad to the bed. I walked away. Mom talked to both of them. I was not sure what she said, but I heard both of them say it would be okay. When I turned around, mom looked as if she was fighting for her last breath. A peaceful look came over her face, then she smiled and closed her eyes.

Mom was buried five days later. It seemed as if she had made all of the arrangements. As I walked away from her grave, I thought about all the sadness that I had had in my life. Michael grabbed my hand and told me that he would always be there for me. He told me that we would be staying there for a while and that Daddy was going back to Dallas with us. Michael grabbed my hand and told me that he would be there for me. He said if it were possible, he would bear this pain for me. I ached deep inside. I had lost my mother. I had lost my friend. Tears rolled down my cheeks. Michael held me closer and closer. He told me that he understood and it would take time for me to heal. He said that there was no loss like the loss of a parent. I grabbed his hand tighter, remembering that he had lost both of his parents too. Michael had suffered also. Michael knew pain. Michael knew disappointment. Michael knew happiness.

The ride to the airport was a sad one. Dad was a little excited because he had never been on a plane. He was sad too because mom was everything to him. He thanked us over and over for taking him with us. Michael told him that he would have it no other way. He told him that he had not only gotten a wife but a dad too. Dad's face glowed so brightly. Sitting on the plane, I thought of Lillian; I thought of Carl; I thought of my mom. I had lost so much, but I believed that I would gain even more with Michael. Michael knew some of the pain I felt. He kissed me and told me that he would love me forever. He told me that I had many earthquakes and tornadoes in my life. He told me that there was always peace after any storm and God was that peace in our life. I smiled and laid back in the arms of my husband.

The alarm went off; I jumped up. I realized that I had spent hours thinking about my past. I got up, got myself together, and started my day.

I was now the pastor's wife and the first lady. I had to be an example, so I had to be on time for the appointment and carry out all the plans Michael and I had made earlier on the telephone. I also had to stop by the nursing home to see Dad.

I looked outside. Yes, the storm was over. Everything appeared so peaceful. All of the rumbling and roaring of the storm had ceased, not only outside but in my life too.

The Lost Locket

Jane woke up early in the morning just to look at the new gold locket that her father had given her for her birthday. Out of all the presents she received, she adored the gold locket most of all. She had seen the same gold locket in Mr. Walker's jewelry store but knew it was almost impossible for her to save up enough money from her weekly allowance to get her heart's desire.

Jane loved her father very much. She was separated from him when she was two, but they were reunited when she turned fourteen. She finally got to know her father. Her stepfather talked badly about her father all the time. He criticized him because he was never able to keep a job, he moved from state to state and never wrote or called but always told his mother (Jane's grandmother) to tell Jane he loved her and how much he thought about her every day. Jane's stepfather said he was saying all of that just to buy her love and keep her thinking of him. Her stepfather hated her father. Her father was not allowed to come to the house so whenever he wanted to see Jane, she had to meet him at the neighborhood store. They would have the best of times. They would share soda pops and chips. They would talk about her desires and dreams. They would walk around and look in store windows and point out all the pretty dresses and jewelry he would buy her. She knew once he got a job, he would do better.

She would sometimes call, but he was either out of town or just leaving. He always had so much to do. Even though Jane's stepfather never had anything good to say about her father, she knew deep inside that she meant the world to her father and that out of the five sisters and two brothers she had never met, he loved and cared for her the most.

Since a lot of her mother's friends had not forgiven him for leaving her mother when she was so young, they never took the time to try to understand his true reasons for leaving home. They had not talked to him. They never knew how much he was hated by his in-laws; they never knew how his in-laws insisted on my mother talking to someone else who was more financially stable. They never knew how they made her mother promise that she would not allow him to father another child and made her divorce him. They never knew how cruel her friends were to him and how it seemed no one ever gave him a chance. They just thought he was disgusting and lazy, but she knew the truth because her father told her things that no one ever asked.

Thinking about this and rubbing the locket gently, Jane remembered the day he left. She heard her mother talking to someone in the kitchen. The walls were thin so she could hear everything they said. Her mother was very angry. She was yelling at the top of her voice. Jane listened closely to see what was wrong. She heard her father's voice also. She wondered what was happening and what was he doing at the house. Her stepfather was at work, and she knew if he were home, he would not allow him to be on the property.

Her mother continued to scream at her father. She told him that he was not going to mess up things for her and her relationship. She said that he had not been around all this time, and he did not need to start something he knew he would not continue. She told him the locket was nice, but that was all he had ever given his daughter. Jane's father tried to explain, but her mother did not listen. Her father asked if he could see his daughter before he left, and she said no. She told him to leave her premises. If not, he would be arrested.

She heard her father slam the door. Her mother opened the door and said that he had messed up her daughter's life, and he would not have another opportunity to continue. He said that he did want to get to know her better, but prior commitments in other states kept him busy. He said that he was glad to have had the chance, but he realized that he could never be a father to any of his children. He said at least all of them have something to remember him by. Softly, he said, "I am sorry. I have to move on in life."

As Jane thought about this incident, tears rolled down her cheeks. She cried and cried. She held her locket, knowing that even though she had received what she thought was her heart's desire, she had lost forever the one who gave her the locket.

There Is Peace In The Valley

One day in the year 1995, life took a drastic change for the better. It was the greatest day of my life. It was the day that I felt all of my sins were forgiven and forgotten. It was the day that I knew God loved me. It was the day that I realized that God would do anything for me.

They were the cutest babies I had ever seen. From the time I laid eyes on them, I knew they would make me happy and their father proud. I knew they were little miracles in our lives. I knew that this was the beginning of even greater things to come, and we were so happy to be parents.

Alan, their father, and I had separated several times before they were born. We had been married for over ten years before we had children. We thought we would never have a child. Alan always seemed to have a hate for me because I could not give him a child, and because I had done something to almost break up our marriage. In our many arguments, he once told me that I was less than a woman; I was a deceiver; and if he had known I could not have children, he would never have married me. Alan was a nice man; everyone cared about him. I really do not know if he had fallen out of love with me or if he was just disappointed in me. His only conversation was how badly he wanted a child. He would tell me about all of the ladies on his job that were pregnant. He would tell me about his family members who had gotten pregnant. Sometimes he would say to me that his marriage would never be fulfilled if he did not have a child. I thought that was our problem, but I realized that there were other things that were hindering our marriage. Strangely as it sounds, I gave him the desire of his heart after visiting many doctors, therapists, taking lots of pills, and praying. Sometimes he acted as if he disliked me. I started thinking Mama was right. She always told me something was wrong with him, but I did not listen. Mama always could see through my boyfriends. She would tell me which one was a good catch and which ones I would need to let go. I would listen to her, but when Alan came along, I felt that I knew him better than she did. Alan, in my opinion, was different than what she thought. In all truthfulness, Alan was not the problem; I was.

I met Alan in high school. He was in the twelfth grade; I was in the ninth. Every girl I knew would almost go crazy when they saw him running up and down the basketball court. Every girl I knew wanted him, but I ended up with him.

One day when I was on my way home, I bumped into him. All my books fell out of my hand, and he picked them up. He asked me if I were okay and he asked me my name. I quickly gave him my name, and he began asking me questions about my classes and where I lived. I answered as quickly as possible and told him that I had to get the bus. He grabbed me by the hand and said he would take me home. All of a sudden, I realized that Alan Johnson wanted to take me home in his white two-seater. I could not believe that Alan Johnson, number 15 on the basketball team, wanted to take me home. Alan Johnson, the top scorer on our high school team who had college coaches begging for him, wanted to take me home. Alan Johnson, the man that every girl in high school wanted to meet, wanted to take me home. I yelled out yes. He smiled and walked me to his almost new car. He opened the door, and I got in. I sat in that comfortable seat and felt like I was the luckiest woman in the world. As he started the car, I looked around to see if anyone saw me. I looked up at his face and saw the handsome man that all the girls saw. Alan was a good-looking man. He had beautiful smooth skin, a thin mustache, the whitest teeth, and dreamy hazel eyes. He had a deep voice that sent chills up and down my spine when he talked. His chest looked better close up than it did when he was running up and down the court.

Alan was the youngest of five boys. All of his brothers were married and doing very well financially. He was truly loved by his mother and father. It seemed as if they gave him everything he wanted. Alan loved his mother and admired his father. He told everyone that his parents were the best in the world. He loved them, and they loved him. Alan was the perfect son and the perfect child in their minds. He was admired by everyone in the neighborhood. Not only was he athletic, but Alan was an honor roll student. He was very smart. He was liked by the students and teachers. He would always say, I don't want anyone to give me grades, I want to work for them. He was a role model for the other basketball players. He was the first one in the library on weekends, and his teammates followed him. Everyone knew that he would become a person that others would admire; all the mothers knew that he would make some girl proud to take his last name. Alan was known and liked by all. He had been on a number of radio talk shows and on television. News reporters would always have him talk about his team's success or failure after the game. He was the team captain, and he loved his leadership role. He was also on the debate team. It was his desire to become a successful lawyer, and he felt the debate team would prepare him for his future.

As I looked at Alan, I wondered if he was just being nice or if he liked me. He looked at me, smiled, and asked me how I was enjoying the ride. He said even though he had just met me, he was enjoying having me in the passenger's seat. He removed his hand from resting on the gear and held my hand. He told me to tell him about myself. I could barely talk. Alan holding my hand was affecting me more than I knew. He said he was waiting, and I finally asked him what he wanted to know. He said everything. He said he wanted to know everything about me.

I told him I was the only child and that my father died when I was two years old and my mother remarried. I told him that I love my parents, and my stepfather was a sweetheart. He was the only father that I knew. I told him that he would do anything for me. I told him that he adopted me when I turned five years old. I told him that I loved school. I wanted a good education, and I had plans to become a biologist or chemist. He said that even though he was an honor student, he needed additional help in chemistry. I told him that I would be available if he needed help. He said that he would call me the next time he had problems. He said he was sure I would help him get an A in chemistry. We both laughed. He asked me if I were hungry. I told him that I was starving, but there was no way I could go anywhere without letting my parents know. I told him that I could possibly be in trouble because I had not told them that I would not be on the bus. I told him that they trusted me, but they would be worried if I did not get home in time. He said that we could go by a drive through and then he would take me home. I told him that that was fine. We got hamburgers, fries, and two large sodas. We stopped by a store, and I telephoned my mother and told her where I was. She asked me who the boy was and said that we would talk when I got home. On the way home, Alan and I ate and talked. He said he was really enjoying his afternoon and wondered if we could do this every Tuesday since that was the only day that he did not have practice. I told him that I would have to check with my parents. I told him that my mom was already a little concerned. He told me that she did not have anything to worry about. He said he was innocent and a good person. He said that most of the guys had their friends to watch them practice. He said that the coach did not mind as long as they were quiet and not interrupting the players. He asked me if I would come sometimes. I told him that I would talk to my mom and that I was sure I would be able to, especially if I could do my homework. He said it would be noisy, but if all else fails, we could go to the library after practice. He finally arrived at my house. My mom was peeking out of the window. He asked me if I thought he should go inside with me and meet my mom. I told him that I thought it would be better for me to talk to both of them first. He told me that he would let me handle my parents. He told me goodbye and said he would see me tomorrow.

I could not get in the house quick enough. I said hello to my mother. She was calling me, but I ran straight to the telephone to call Darlene. Darlene was my best friend. She was like a sister, and since I did not have one, I adopted her as my play sister. We could talk about everything and everybody. We had no secrets. Darlene and I were the same age, but I was four months older. I was born in January, and she was born in May. I met Darlene in the third grade. We were in the same class. One day our teacher told us to pick a partner to work on a project. I picked Darlene, and we have been friends ever since. After that, our parents met. They became friends, which made our friendship even stronger. Her parents, Mr. and Mrs. Rogers, adored me, and my parents loved Darlene. Darlene was over my house almost every weekend. She was very intelligent. She was well liked by her peers and was known to speak her mind. Whatever was on her mind, she said it loud and clear. She was in the honors class and had the highest average in math in the sixth, seventh, eighth, and ninth grades. I had the highest average in English in the seventh grade. Darlene was so nice. She was always there for me. She was a true friend. She would listen and tell me how she felt whether I wanted to hear it or not. When Darlene was not studying math, she was looking through women magazines, bridal magazines, or magazines that showed home improvements. She desired to be a stay at home mom. No matter how much I would talk to her about leaving our small town and going to college, she would insist that she was going to be the best "stay at home mom" in the area. I told her that she could study math or become a math teacher. She said that she was not interested in college or anything else. I could not get her to change her mind.

Darlene answered the telephone. She sounded as if she was just waking up from a nap. She took a nap every afternoon. I asked her if she was just waking up. She told me that she had not been asleep, but she was very tired. She asked me if I was okay. I told her that I had great news. She asked me to talk quickly. I began telling her about Alan. I told her how I met him and how I had spent the afternoon with him riding in his white two-seater car. She yelled, I yelled, and she begged me to tell her more. I told her that he asked me to come by some afternoons and watch him practice. Darlene was screaming on the telephone. She said she was glad that I had gotten Alan Johnson. She asked me what the other girls were going to say. She told me that they would hate me forever. We both laughed. She said she could not wait to see their faces. I knew Darlene was happy. I could trust Darlene with the news, and I could trust her with Alan. Darlene was a good friend. She was not one that was interested in trying to talk to Alan. She was only interested in my happiness. That is the way I felt about her. She just wanted to make sure that he was treating me fairly and that he cared for me. That was the same way I felt about her with Troy. Darlene said she wanted to tell Troy. Troy and Darlene had been dating for two years. He played football. He was the quarterback and had all types of certificates, trophies, and awards. He was a senior and had already been accepted to an Ivy League college in the south. Troy knew Alan. Darlene was sure that they would become friends now. We talked for hours. We talked about how we would double date, go to the movies, hang out, and just have fun. Time was slipping away, and I still had to do my homework. My mom had come to my room twice, and I still had to talk to her. I told Darlene I would talk to her the next day. She said that she would see if the four of us could go out together Saturday night. She said that she was going to call Troy and see what he was doing. She was so excited she forgot to say goodnight. All of a sudden, I heard a dial tone. I smiled; I knew she was on a mission.

I went to talk to my mom and she told me that she would talk to me in the morning. I said okay. The telephone rang. I picked it up quickly. I asked Darlene what was wrong. The voice on the other end said, "I am not Darlene." It was Alan. I almost lost my breath. He asked me if I was asleep. I told him I was still awake. He asked me about my conversation with my mother. I told him that we were going to talk later. I asked him how he got my number, and he told me that he had his ways. He said that he did not want to talk long, but he just wanted to thank me for a lovely afternoon. I almost fainted. He asked if he could see me at lunchtime. I told him that I would be in the cafeteria. He said he would see me. He said he was going to find a way to get out of class. I asked him if he wanted to go out Saturday night. He said that was wonderful. I told him that I would check with my parents. I also asked if we could go out with another couple. He said if I got permission to go out, he would pick me up and we would meet the other couple. I told him I had to finish my homework. He thanked me again and said he would see me the next day.

I saw Alan every day. I don't know how he was able to eat lunch with me. I am not sure how he was able to get out of class. Darlene was right. I had a lot of girls rolling their eyes at me. I felt like a queen laughing and talking with a king. Darlene and I talked every night about Alan. I could not wait for Saturday night. Troy was looking forward to it also. He kept telling Darlene that maybe he and Alan would end up being friends since both of them were dating great women.

I had spent the whole week with Alan and having him meet my mother and father was the icing on the cake. They seemed to like him, but I knew they were waiting for our first date to be over before they gave me their true opinion about him. The plans were that Alan would drive over to my house, park his car, and we would ride with Darlene and Troy. We could not ride with Alan unless he borrowed his father's car. His two-seater would not have enough room. I was okay with riding with Darlene and Troy, and so was Alan. We just wanted to be together.

Alan knocked on the door around eight o'clock. I was so excited that while going to the door, I tripped over my stepfather's shoe and fell down. My stepfather helped me up and told me to have a seat. He opened the door. Alan looked so handsome standing at the door. I could not believe that this good-looking man was going to be my date. Being a gentleman at all times, he introduced himself and shook my stepfather's hand. He asked about my mother and then looked at me. He spoke to me and told me how adorable I looked. He thanked my stepfather for allowing him to take me out. I listened and knew then that his smooth talking would cause my parents to adore him also. My mother walked in, and he spoke to her. He immediately began asking them about their day. He told them that his parents were looking forward to meeting them. My stepfather asked him about his father, and before the conversation ended, my stepfather said he thought he knew him. My mother was smiling so hard and enjoying the conversation that she did not hear her timer go off. She was baking a pie. I had to call her twice to remind her that she needed to turn it off and take the pie out of the oven. She finally went into the kitchen. Alan told my stepfather that he had a lovely daughter and that he was pleased that he had met a lovely lady. My stepfather smiled and began telling him my life history. He told him about when I was in girl scouts, dance school, drama club, etc. Finally, there was another knock on the door. It was Troy and Darlene.

Darlene came in, spoke to my parents, spoke to Alan, and introduced Troy to Alan. She then looked at me and said, "Let's go." I got up. My stepfather got up and told us to have a good time. My mom came out of the kitchen and told us not to stay out too late. We all said okay. Alan grabbed my hand as we were walking out of the doorway and asked me how I was doing. I told him that I was okay. I told him that once we got in the car, we would have more time to talk. I told him that he did a good job entertaining my parents. He laughed and opened the car door for me. Darlene and Troy were in the car, waiting for us. They had decided where we would go and what we would do since Alan and I could not make up our mind. Darlene had the evening planned just like I knew she would. We ate dinner, went to a play, talked, and laughed. We talked in the car and in the park. Troy and Alan talked about sports and their coaches; Darlene and I talked about Alan and what she thought of him. Darlene talked about our weddings and how many children we would have. She told me that after she and Troy got married, she would be my wedding planner. Darlene had really gotten involved with all of this. I had to stop her and remind her that we were on a date with the men in our lives and not talking on the telephone. She laughed and said she was glad that the guys did not hear her.

That night was the beginning of the rest of my life. Alan graduated from high school and went to play basketball for a school in the Washington, D.C., area. I was still in high school and was hoping that I was not going to get a letter telling me that he had met someone new. I just knew what he said he was feeling for me was going to leave. My feeling for him grew stronger and stronger. I would see him on television, and when the reporters would finish talking to him, he would say hello to me. Darlene would always call after she saw him and ask me how I was feeling. We would talk about how we thought he felt about me. She and Troy were doing fine. Troy was in college, but he was not on television as much as Alan. The girls hated me more and more. I just continued to smile, do my work, and wait for spring break and the end of the school year.

As our senior year came to an end, Troy and Darlene began to ask me more questions about my feelings for Alan. Alan was now a junior in college. All he talked about was graduating and going to law school. He was getting a lot of professional offers to play basketball, but he continued to say he wanted to be a lawyer. His parents were in favor of his decision. Even my parents felt that he had a right to make a decision about his future.

I graduated from high school and was getting ready to enter college. Alan had graduated early and was entering law school. We had been friends at that time, and I think everyone saw that our love was getting deeper and deeper. I think I was waiting for the proposal. Mom and Dad started telling me it was important for me to get a career before I got married. My mom kept telling me to travel, enjoy myself, and make some money before I thought about getting married. She told me that she liked Alan, but it was just something about him. She said she was not sure what, but there was something that was keeping her from feeling that he was the guy for me. I would just smile at her. I knew my mom would think of something. Alan was still Alan to me. He loved me; I could tell. He would come home, call me, take me out, visit Darlene and Troy, visit my parents, take me to see his parents, and leave. He did not hang out with anyone else because he was spending his time with me. Even Troy and Darlene felt that he was serious. He had begun to tell me more and more how he felt and question me about my feelings for him. I told him how I felt and he would always say that he needed to know. He would write me, call, and even visit me at college. This went on the whole time I was in college and he was in law school. We started spending lots of time together. I felt I was the only woman in his life except for his mother. I was very happy.

When he graduated from law school and passed the law exam, Alan threw himself a big party. He invited all his family, coaches, friends, my family, Darlene, and Troy. He also invited some of his professors. He told me that he was celebrating my graduation also. Both of us were so happy. He could not wait for the party. He wanted everything just right. During the party, he was so friendly and happy. Darlene and Troy were having a ball. They were enjoying themselves and talking about all the money, time, and energy he had put in this celebration. Darlene and Troy had graduated from college, and they were celebrating as if it was their party also. I just wanted all of us to be happy.

Alan stopped the music and thanked everyone for his friendship. I was standing beside him, smiling. He said that he wanted to thank me for working hard to make sure that the party was a success. I smiled. He said he had one more announcement. At that time, I looked at him because I was thinking he was going to thank his parents. He looked at me and asked me to marry him. I did not know what to do. I looked at him, at the people, at Darlene, and at my mom. I saw Darlene shaking her head up and down, and I finally got myself together to say yes. He hugged me like never before. He whispered in my ear that I had made him a happy man. Everyone applauded and said congratulations.

I left the party with Alan. I knew I loved him, but I really wanted to know how my parents felt and how Darlene felt. His parents were happy. They always told me that they wanted me to be their daughter-in-law. They had adopted me as their daughter, and his brother had been calling me sister.

I got home that morning. My parents were in the kitchen eating breakfast. They kissed me and said that we had their blessings. My mom said that maybe she was wrong. My mother said she wanted me to have lunch with her the next day because there were things we had to talk about. I agreed and went to my room. I called Darlene. Darlene said she was waiting by the telephone all night. Darlene asked me how I was feeling. I told her I was okay. She asked me if I was sure that I wanted to marry Alan. Before I could answer that question, she asked me if I loved him. I told her that I loved him. She asked me what I was going to do about my career. She said that she was sure that Alan had his life planned. I think she asked me every question she could think of. Some questions I could answer and some I could not. She told me that I did not have to answer all of them, but think about them before I got married. She told me that I was her friend forever and whatever decision I made she would be there for me. I got off the telephone puzzled because I could not understand the questions. I guess reality had hit for all of us.

I thought about all the questions she asked. I thought about Alan, and I thought about Josh. Josh was my best-kept secret. He was a guy I met in college. He was in one of my classes and my study group. He was my roommate's brother. After class, a group of us would go out and get something to eat. He was always saying how much he liked me, but I told him all about Alan. He would always say that Alan was not the right man for me. We would laugh about that, but I always told Josh that Alan was going to be my husband. We became good friends. He would tell me about his girlfriend and some of the problems they had. Alan knew about Josh. He knew we were friends, and when he visited, he would see Josh. What he did not know was how close Josh and I had gotten. Josh ended his relationship with his girlfriend because she told him that she wanted to date someone else. Josh was heartbroken. I was there for him. We became close friends after that. I tried to help him by spending time with him and trying to make him do things to keep his mind off of her. I did not want Josh depressed. We started going out together, going to the movies and some parties. I spent a couple of weekends at his parents' house. Both times I went with my roommate. I was not aware that Josh had plans to be home one weekend I went, nor did I know that his parents were out of town. His sister always had plans that she never shared so one weekend she went to the beach. Josh and I were together that weekend.

Josh was the man that I always wanted to tell Darlene about. Alan did not know that when he was not visiting me, I was spending my time with Josh. I had introduced Darlene to him when she visited me during the summer. I took a couple of classes for the summer because Josh had gotten a job. I wanted to spend my summer with him. Darlene thought Josh was cute, but she had no idea that Josh was becoming the other man in my life. Darlene wanted to know why I was not coming home as much, but I did not know how to tell her about Josh. I felt bad, because I had never kept a secret from Darlene. I did not feel she would understand.

Josh was tall. He had dark brown hair and blue eyes. His eyes were beautiful. He had dimples. He was cute. I never expected to fall in love with him. He was such a nice person. We would talk about everything. He was concerned about me and my needs. He adored me. We talked about our feelings, his parents, friends, and our future. He was comical. He was always making jokes. He was very smart. He was always creating inventions; he had a patent on a couple of them. His parents were very supportive financially. Josh loved to travel. He would always tell me about the places he and his family had been.

Josh knew a lot about me. He knew all about Alan too. I had told him everything. He felt Alan did not love me the way he did. He said that Alan was concerned about himself. He said that if Alan ever hurt me, he would be there for me. We did everything together. We went camping, fishing, and even scuba diving. I visited his family often. They knew I had a boyfriend, but they were sure the relationship would be over soon.

I loved Josh. The night before I graduated, I laid in his arms and cried because I felt I would never see him again. I had spent a lot of my college years with him. We had been able to do things together and go places without any of my family members, friends, and even my boyfriend knowing about it. I had been able to get out of appointments home, get off the telephone with Darlene, and even change the times Alan was coming to see me, based on a final examination, a project, a seminar, extra homework, or meeting a study group. Darlene even joked about the degree I was getting. She was wondering what degree was taking me away from my friends and family. She said she thought her major was difficult, but she was glad she did not choose the one I had chosen. She said, "You are really committed to your classes; I hope they pay off." I just could not tell her about Josh. I wanted to, and I tried so many times. I just felt she would not say what I wanted to hear. I did not want her to tell me how she felt Alan loved me and how she felt he was faithful. I did not want to hear any statements about Josh and his family.

Josh gave me a bracelet to always remember him. He told me that he would always keep me in his heart. He asked me to tell Alan about him. He asked me to leave Alan. He promised me that no matter our differences, our love would conquer all. I smiled and thought about our differences. I wondered how my parents would handle that. They would probably be okay, but it would be a problem for some. It didn't matter though, I really loved him. We did not have any problems in college, and his parents were so accepting. Josh held me so close and asked me if I realized that this was goodbye. We both cried, but I told him I had to go. Alan was on his way. He was supposed to have arrived at the airport at ten, rent a car, and check in the hotel and meet me at the bookstore at one o'clock. It was twelve thirty, so I told Josh I had to go. He smiled and asked what I would do if he walked over with me. I asked him not to. He hugged me and said goodbye.

As I sat there reminiscing, I realized that my wedding was one week away. Darlene and Troy were in the wedding. She was my maid of honor, and Troy was Alan's best man. They had become good friends. They were almost like brothers. Darlene and Troy had moved to Canada and were planning on getting married next year. They were really a great couple. They would do anything for us, and we would do anything for them. I had to tell Darlene my secret. I felt like I had betrayed her. I felt like I had committed a crime and needed to confess. I promised myself that the day one of us got married, I would tell her. Darlene had been down one time to help me prepare for the wedding, but the words never came out. I could not keep this secret; we were more than friends; we were like sisters.

At five o'clock, I was at the airport waiting patiently to pick up Darlene and Troy. Darlene ran out to hug me, and Troy followed. We embraced. Darlene starting talking about the flight, Troy and the man on the plane, the little girl that was in the next row, etc. I stopped her and told her we had to talk later. She said okay and started the whole conversation again. She finally stopped and asked about what; she wanted to know if there were problems with the wedding. I assured her that everything was on schedule. She immediately turned to Troy and started talking about picking up the luggage. Troy walked ahead of us. She asked me if I had gotten all of the items she asked me to get and if I had all of the appointments. I looked at her and told her all of the arrangements and appointments had been scheduled. I also told her that my parents, Alan's parents, and Alan had been very helpful in helping me complete all of my tasks. We got the luggage, picked up the car, and dropped Troy off at the hotel. Alan was picking him up later. Darlene told me that everything was going great with them and they had started planning their wedding. She said her mother was happy because she was not pleased with their living arrangements. Darlene was so excited for me. She asked if I wanted to go eat before we got started with everything and I told her okay. We had a great time at the restaurant. The waiter flirted with us, and we did the same with him. We had a great time, and the food was delicious. We talked about everything.

After about fifty minutes, I told Darlene I had something to tell her. Before I could talk, she asked me if I was pregnant. I told her no. She said she could not think of anything else. It was then that I told her about Josh. She asked me if it was the guy that she met when I was in college. I told her yes. She asked me if I had been in contact with him since I had left college. I told her that I had not seen him, but I had called his parents' house and told them about the wedding. She asked me if I needed medical attention. She looked at me with such disgust. She told me she needed a minute. We both sat quietly at the table. I just looked at her. She spoke almost in a whisper when she asked me what Alan said. I told her that I had not told him. She raised her voice and asked if I was going to marry him with this news hanging over my head. The people at the next table looked at us. I ask her to lower her voice and then told her that Alan did not have to know. I was thinking to myself; I was sorry I told her. I expected a reaction, but not this one. I told her that Alan would never know and I wanted her to keep this secret like everything else. Darlene looked at me as if I were a stranger. She told me to think about what I was doing and did I want this to happen to me. I told her that I had not and would not give this information that much thought. She asked me if I had told my mother. I told her no, and I did not expect her to tell her. I told her that it was ironic that my mother continued to tell me to watch out for him, but I was the one he needed to watch. Darlene paid the check and was ready to go.

We rode in silence for about thirty minutes. Finally, Darlene said my secret was safe with her. She said she forgave me for taking so long to tell her. She said that she would always be a true friend and sister. She said she wanted me to be happy and made me promise that I did not have any more secrets. I told her that Josh was out of my life and that our relationship was over. I told her that I had heard that Josh had met a nice young lady and was engaged to be married. She told me I needed to put closure on everything, even the connection with his family. I laughed and told her I would.

It was the most beautiful wedding I had ever seen. I felt like I was an observer more than a participant. Everything was lovely. I was in white and cried through the whole ceremony; so did Darlene. I am not sure what she was crying about, but I was happy. Alan was more handsome than ever. He was the man for me. I did not want this moment to cease. We laughed, we danced, and did all the things you do at a wedding. Darlene caught the bouquet. I made sure of that and so did she. Troy got the garter. Alan had worked that out with Troy. He knew how to position himself to catch it. I guess his football days paid off. I smiled the whole time. It was the best wedding I had ever attended. My parents were happy; Alan's parents' were happy; and my friends were happy. I was the most beautiful bride ever. The pictures just did not tell the story of how great everything looked.

The honeymoon was fantastic. We spent two weeks in Hawaii. We were on a secluded island. I don't know how Alan got it, and I did not care. I did not want to leave. It was everything I had imagined and then more. It seemed as if nothing could ever go wrong in my life. I was happier than I ever thought I could be. I loved my husband.

We arrived in Michigan at five in the morning. Alan had made all the arrangements so I would be seeing our house for the first time. The movers had taken care of everything. I would miss Chicago, but I knew I had to make this change. Darlene and Troy were back in Canada, and I was not too far from them. I knew my life could only get better even though I had to find a job. Alan was okay. He had a job before he left, and he was ready to start practicing law in a new state and city. He was very doing great. We were happy, and everything was moving along so smoothly. Alan was the perfect husband, and I was the perfect wife. We were having a great time. Marriage could not have gotten any better. I was on top of the mountain, and he was standing right beside me. Everything was great.

I started my job in October. I was working at one of the local universities. House worked slowly came to an end. I was not waiting at the door for my husband as before. Sometimes I got home after Alan. We had date nights, and we spent our weekends together. We went on trips and, when I could get off, I went on some of Alan's business trips. Alan loved bowling, so some nights, we went bowling. He was really good and was seriously considering joining a league. Things had changed some, but our marriage was beautiful.

Three years went by, and I was thinking more and more about Josh. Alan was working late into the night, and I was leaving early in the morning to get my day started and catch up on work that was waiting and piling up on my desk. We had an argument almost every day. I was married to a successful lawyer, living in my dream house, had a great job, and had great investments, but something was going wrong. I had been talking to Darlene about the situation. She told me to just relax. She and Troy were doing great. Their wedding was beautiful. It was what I expected and more. We had spent a couple of holidays with them, and life seemed to be great. You could tell Troy and Darlene really loved each other. Darlene would always pull me in a corner or in the basement and ask me if I had heard from Josh. I reminded her that the relationship was over. She would just say good keep it that way.

Alan lost his father. He had a heart attack. Alan's world went upside down. He took off two weeks from work just to get himself together. He had a hard time coping, and I was there for him every step of the way. He thanked me almost every day for being the wife that I was. He said that he had been thinking about a lot of things. He was glad that his mother had gone to live with her sister. He said that it seemed as if his family was getting smaller and smaller. I told him that everything would be okay. He looked at me and then asked if I was ready to start a family. I smiled and said I was enjoying my life. I told him that I had gotten a promotion on my job, I was traveling more, and he had moved up in his job, so maybe this was not the right time. He looked at me rather sadly and said I promised him after three years of marriage that we would start a family. I looked at him in shock because I thought he had forgotten about that; I had. Alan and I talked, but you could tell our lives changed from that moment. Our lives became routine. He would come in, eat, watch television, or read the paper. I would come in, eat, and read a book. We would talk, but mostly about work or about something Darlene and Troy were doing. This worked for me for a while. It gave me more time to think about Josh, but I could tell our marriage was suffering. One night when he came home, I asked him if he really wanted a child. He told me that he always wanted a child, but he wanted to respect my wishes. He said that he felt he would be a good father and he knew he was a good provider. I agreed with him. He looked so sad. He told me that he wanted to have a child like Darlene and Troy. He said he wanted to be more than a godfather, he wanted to be a father. Darlene and Troy had a six-month-old little girl. We got pictures from them almost every day. I think every picture Alan saw made him want a baby more and more. I guess I wanted a child, but I did not want one then. I was fine being godmother and not a mother. I loved my godchild, but I was not sure if I could love one of my own. I looked at Alan. I kissed him and told him that we would try. He was so happy. We started then.

A year had passed, and Alan decided to go to the doctor. He told me that he was sure it was something wrong with him. I told him that maybe we were trying too hard. Maybe we needed to take it easy and just let things happen. He went to the doctor and found out that he was okay. He came home and said it was my time. I told him that I was sure I was fine but if that would make him happy I would go. He could not wait to go with me that morning. He was ready before I was. I guess he was determined to find out what the problem was and I am sure by this time he thought it was me. We went in and talked to the doctor about our situation. He assured Alan that I was not the problem. Jokingly, the doctor said maybe one of you really don't want to get pregnant. I laughed; Alan looked at me with disgust. The doctor told us to go back and work on things.

Alan was quiet in the car. He was driving rather aggressively. I asked him what was wrong. He told me if I did not want a child, I should have told him. He said that he agreed with the doctor. He knew I was the one that did not want a child. He told me that he was disappointed in me and if he knew I felt that way that maybe he should not have married me. He said he had turned down many women before and during our marriage just because he was faithful to me. He said that if he had known how I really felt maybe he would have had a couple of kids out of wedlock and taken some of those women up on their offer even after he had gotten married. He said, "If you continue this foolishness, then maybe I will." I did not say anything. He continued to fuss all the way home. The more he talked, the more he said things that I could not believe he was saying. We had been married four years, and this was the first night that I slept alone. I moved into the guest room. Alan slept in our bedroom. I was lonesome; I missed him, but I decided to let Alan get over his frustration. I knew if I had said anything, it would have ended this marriage. I wanted to tell him about Josh and how I would have willingly had his children.

The next morning, I had breakfast on the table, but Alan did not eat. After work, my mother called and asked me what was wrong with Alan. She said that he called his mother and told her the whole story. I thought Alan was going through something, but this was too much. I could not wait for Alan to come home. As soon as he walked into the house, we had the biggest argument. Both of us said things we regretted, and both of us knew that a separation was in order. Alan said that he needed some time, so he was going to Denver for a couple of weeks. He left the address and telephone number on the kitchen table. He went into our bedroom and packed his bags. He said his plane left in two hours. I told him to enjoy his trip, and hopefully, I would be there when he got back. He looked at me and said he needed some time to think and make some decisions.

News traveled fast. My mom called me about thirty minutes later very upset. She told me that Alan was less than a man. She said that she knew something was wrong with him. She said that she was so sorry I married him. She said that anyone that had to leave town to work out his problem had problems.

She said that he and his mother had issues. I told her that Alan had to do what he had to do, and I had to do what I had to do. After all the fussing, she told me to call him and see if I could put some sense in his head. She apologized for saying all those things about Alan and told me that she was upset. She told me that if I wanted to come back home, she and my stepfather would be waiting with open arms.

I called Darlene and told her about the situation. She was sad but asked me what my problems were. She said that having a baby should not be a problem for me. It was simple. All I needed to do was have a baby. She said she understood how Alan felt, and it was up to me to get myself together and save my marriage. I listened but thought Darlene had bumped her head. She continued telling me that I needed to get myself together and beg my husband to come back home. After her long conversation, she told me she loved me, and if I needed to call her, she would be there for me. I thanked her and said goodbye. I knew after that telephone call that I had to do something. There was one thing about Darlene, no matter how direct and no matter how much she fussed, she made good sense, and I needed to listen.

Weeks passed, and I did not hear from Alan, nor did I call him. I was working overtime, resting, praying, thinking, going out with co-workers, and talking to my mother and Darlene. I had made up my mind that once Alan came back, I would focus and give him the baby he wanted. I loved my husband, and I wanted to give him a baby as well as have a part of us in the world. I was so happy about my decision. I made plans to make Alan's arrival the most romantic night ever. I called him, and he answered the phone on the first ring. He said he was a fool to say the things he had said. He apologized. He said he was wrong and asked me to forgive him for being so immature. He said he missed me and wanted to come home. He said since I did not call, he thought I had left. He said he was afraid to call and was dreading coming home to an empty house. I told him that I did not leave. I was home and wanted him to come home. He said he would do whatever he could do to get the next flight out. He said he loved me and put the telephone down. He called back in about forty minutes to say that he had made all the necessary arrangement and would be home at 7:00 p.m. the next day. I was smiling. I was so happy. I could not wait for my man to come home.

Alan arrived, and our night together was better than our honeymoon. Alan and I were so happy. Since he had gotten back, every day was wonderful. I started to believe that both of us needed the separation. Alan was great. He was the perfect husband. We had talked to both of our parents and Darlene. Everyone was happy that we had made up and were staying together. Two months later, I was pregnant.

Alan was so happy. He did everything he could to make me comfortable. If he could have picked me up and taken me around, he would have. Everything was going fine until I fell.

It was a snowy day. I was on my way to work. Alan has insisted on driving me, but I told him that I would be okay. I walked out of the house to get in the car and missed my step. I fell on my face. The cement steps felt as if they were stuck in my stomach. I could not move. I tried to yell, but the pain was unbearable. All I could do was cry and hope my baby was okay. I had grown so attached to my baby. I did not know how I could fall in love so quickly with a baby that I had not even seen. After a minute or so, I was able to yell for Alan. I did not know where he was. I yelled again. Finally, he ran out of the house. Blood was all over the place. He started crying, telling me that I would be okay. He picked me up and put me in the car. We arrived at the hospital in what seemed to be ten minutes, and we were thirty minutes away. I was having severe pains. I felt that I was going to faint at any minute. The doctors ran out and put me on a bed. All I saw were lights. When I opened my eyes two days later, I was in another room. Alan and Troy were in the corner. My mom and Darlene were standing over me. My stepfather was looking out the window, and Alan's mother was looking in the mirror. The doctor was standing on the opposite side. He took my hand and told me that I had lost my baby. I just cried and cried. Alan hugged me, and we cried together. My mom told me that I would be okay. Darlene said she would spend a couple of days with me to make sure that I was okay.

Alan and I walked around the house like zombies for months. We finally got ourselves together after seeing a therapist. She was able to help us feel like living again and feel good about trying to have another baby.

One year later, Dr. Toppes verified the home pregnancy test. I was one month pregnant. Alan and I were so happy. Alan pulled out the crib again. He had put it in the basement and had talked about giving it to his cousin. Alan was happy. He continued to tell me that God has given us another chance to raise a child. Everyone was happy for us. Darlene came down periodically to see how I was doing. The people at work constantly watched me to make sure I was okay. About 3:00 a.m. in my fifth month, I woke up in blood. Alan did not know what was wrong. He rushed me to the hospital; I lost twins. Dr. Toppes was shocked. He said he had not seen the other child. Alan could not handle the loss.

Life was not the same for us. Alan stayed angry all the time. He barely noticed me in the bedroom. Darlene and Troy visited. Darlene asked me what was wrong. I told her that we both were frustrated. She suggested that we see a therapist. I told her that we had done that and I was not sure if Alan wanted to do that again. Darlene said she would talk to Alan. Alan said he did not want to see another therapist and he did not want to see me. He said that I was the cause of everything. If I had told him that I did not want a family, it would have been okay. He told her that he wondered if I did something to lose his babies. He said that everything seemed so strange. Darlene became very upset with Alan. I talked to Alan, and he told me the same thing. He asked me to leave the house, or he would leave. I left with Darlene and Troy that night. I stayed with them for about two weeks. Then I rented a small apartment about ten miles from my house. I took a leave of absence from my job. I needed time too. I told Darlene and Troy that I needed my own space. They insisted that I stay with them, but I told them no. Alan and I stayed in touch. I did not get the apology like I did before, but he said that we could at least talk to each other. We talked every week. Alan was working overtime and almost every weekend. He would call every week and talk about his job, us, and the new addition he wanted to put on the house. He had asked me if he could come to see me, but I told him that I thought it would be better if we continued the separation for a while longer. I loved him and missed him, but the separation was good for both of us.

Friday night was my night to go to my favorite restaurant. The waiter knew me, and he knew what I wanted to eat. He would ask every week if I was expecting someone else and I would say no. He would look at me and say one night he was going to eat with me. I sat there thinking and decided to call Alan and invite him over. I called, but he was not at home. I ate and enjoyed my meal.

I worked hard on my job. Every now and then I think my supervisor thought she was rewarding me by sending me on a business trip. I had been to Texas a couple of times and then she decided to send me to Canada for two months. Canada was fine. It was truly the place to go to stop thinking about Alan. During my stays there I had found this fabulous restaurant. I was going almost every Friday night like I was doing when

I was at home. I thought that the most I could do was eat my problem away and I did. The food at this restaurant was fantastic. I would see couples come in and think about Alan and me, but I had already started thinking that eventually our marriage would be over.

I sat there thinking, and then I decided to call Alan. He did not answer, so I called his mother's house and he was there eating dinner. I talked to him for about fifteen minutes, hung up the telephone, and began eating my meal. The meal was delicious. The waiter came by to see if I needed anything. I was okay, but after he left, I realized I needed another cup of coffee I looked back to call him and then I saw him. I saw Josh. He was sitting all alone at the table behind me drinking coffee. He had gotten older and was looking better than he did in college. He had a beard, his brown hair was cut close and neatly, and he had gotten bigger and muscular. His blue eyes looked as if they were dancing under his eyelids. I just looked at him and stared. I thought I could just keep eating, and he would not even know I was here. I knew it was wrong, but I could not resist. I walked to the table and said hello. He almost choked on his coffee. He stared at me and told me I was more beautiful than ever. He kissed me on my hand and told me to take a seat. I smiled and told him that I was at the next table. He jumped up and said that he would join me. He followed me to the table. He said that he could not believe that he was sitting in front of me. He asked me if this was for real or if he was dreaming. I told him that it was real. He asked me what I was doing in Canada. I told him that I was on a business trip and visiting my best friend. He asked me how life was treating me, and how was my husband. Before I could answer, he told me he was divorced. He said he had no children, and he was still in love with me. I looked at him. I told him that Alan and I had been separated for a couple of months. I told him that I could possibly stay because my company had a small branch in Canada. He told me that after divorcing his wife, he was depressed and lonely. He moved to Canada. He did not sell his house; he gave it to her. He bought a new one and had been there for three years. He told me he had room if I needed a place to stay. I smiled and kept talking. I reminded him that my girlfriend lived in Canada also. Talking to Josh was just like old times. I told him about the three babies I had lost. He said he was sorry and that he wished he had been there with me. I told him that Alan was the perfect husband I asked him what happened to his marriage. He told me that he left her because he did not love her. He said he loved me. He said that he was so in love with me that he got a tattoo that would always remind him of me. He rolled up his sleeve, and LAURA was on his arm. I could not believe he had my name on his arm. The waiter came by, and I told him we were okay. He looked at me and said, "Your friend came. Was he the one you were looking for? I could not imagine a beautiful woman sitting alone without someone coming to meet her." I looked at him and said yes. He smiled and left. I asked Josh why he put my name on his arm. I asked him if he was drunk. He said he was sober, and this was the only way he could let the world know how much he loved me. He told me that he missed me and he thought about me all the time. He said he thought about me when he was with his wife. I looked puzzled. He told me that he was a man in love. I looked at Josh and asked if he wanted some of my meal. He smiled and said the coffee was fine. He asked me where I was staying. I told him that I was renting an apartment. I gave him the name of the apartment building, and he said that he owned that building. He said that I could stay there as long as I wanted. He would take care of everything. He also reminded me of all of the space he had in his house. I did not respond. He told me that he was in real estate and had been buying property since he left college. He paid the bill and tipped the waiter, and we left.

He insisted on taking me home. He said no cab for me. If anyone was going to chauffer, it would be him. The drive home was a quiet one and a quick one. Before I knew it, we were parked in front of the apartment building. He asked me if he could come by sometimes and visit. He said that he knew I was still married and he would respect my situation. I told him that I would let him know. He asked if he could have my number. I gave it to him. He said he wanted to spend more time with me. I opened the car door and got out before he jumped out of the car. He said he would call me in the morning. I ran into the house and locked the door. There was no way I could let Josh come in or stop by. I was a married woman and I loved Alan no matter how crazy he was acting. I sat nervously on the bed. I called Alan, but he did not answer. I called Darlene. I was not going to keep another secret. I told her what had happened. She was very quiet on the telephone. She asked me if I wanted to move back in with her and Troy. I told her that I was a married woman, and I would carry myself that way. She told me to call Alan and see if he could come up for the weekend. I told her that I would call him in the morning. Darlene told me to call her if I needed her. She told me to call her if I felt like getting in trouble or if I was in trouble. I told her that it was good seeing Josh, but my relationship with him was over. She said she would talk to me in the morning.

There was a knock on the door. I looked at the clock, and it was 1:45 a.m. I was frightened. I sat up in my bed and asked who was at the door. The voice said, "Josh." I ran to the door and let him in. I forgot how I was dressed. Josh looked at me and told me that I looked gorgeous. He said that he really enjoyed seeing me. I said it was good seeing him too. He said he was great, and he did not want to leave town without saying goodbye. I asked him where he was going. He said he would be in Missouri for about five months working on a project. He said he wanted to say goodbye. He kissed me so gently and then held me in his strong arms. He said he wished that he was my husband and the mother of his children. He told me that he loved me and that he did not want to spend his last night in town alone. By this time, Alan was far from my mind. All the feelings I had for Josh came back. I reached out for his hand and walked into the bedroom.

He kissed me on my forehead and said good night. He told me that he was not going to come between a man and his wife, but he loved me more than Alan. When my eyes opened, I could only think of Josh. I turned over to say good morning, but all I found was a note. The note said, "My golden lady, you looked so peaceful, I did not want to wake you; I will call you as soon as I get settled." I looked at the clock and it was eleven o'clock. I was really shocked. I had overslept. I grabbed the telephone and called the office. Tony, answered the telephone. I told him to tell Cane, the director, that I would be in around one o'clock. I jumped in the shower and thought about Josh, Alan, and then Darlene. I did not know what to do. I had to talk to Darlene, but how could I tell Alan. I had to talk to Josh. I had just realized what I had done.

Work was so peaceful. I left at six. I could not wait to call Darlene. I ran into the house and headed for the shower. I thought for a moment that Josh was in the bathroom, but then I realized he was gone. I swung the door open, and Alan was standing in the shower. He had a big smile on his face. He said he had been talking to Darlene about how lonely I was. He said he talked to several people, and they made him realize that he was wrong. He told me that he was sorry. He said that he did not call because he wanted to surprise me. He said he felt if he told me, I probably would suggest that more time was needed. He said he had learned his lesson and he was tired of being alone. He said that Darlene took care of all the arrangements.

153

He said that she had just left minutes before I came in. He said she let him in and gave him the keys. She said she talked to the apartment manager and they were all up for surprising you.

At that moment, the telephone rang. I ran to answer it. Josh said hello and began telling me how much he loved me. I told him that Alan came up unannounced. He laughed and said he was glad he had left. I told him that I did not know what his visit would mean. Josh said he understood and reminded me that I had his address and telephone number. He told me to call anytime. He said he would be waiting. I ran back to the bathroom. Alan asked if I was talking to Darlene or my boyfriend. He looked at me and asked me why I was still dressed. He started to undress me. I told him that I was tired and I needed time to think about our separation and his visit. He said he understood, but he was not the man that left. He asked me to forgive him. He said he knew it would take time, but that was all he had.

Two weeks passed. Josh had not called. I came home frustrated and tired from work. Alan came out of the bathroom and kissed me. He thanked me for my love and for being such a special lady. He said he wanted to start over. He said he wanted our life to be like it was the first three years of our marriage. I did not know what to say. He told me that he was okay with us never having a baby. If we wanted to, we could adopt. He said that the distance made him think and realize that he did not want to be in this world or a state without me. I looked at him and thought about Josh. He said that he was thinking about moving to Canada. He said that he had a lot of plans that he wanted to share, but first he wanted to show me how much he missed me. Before I knew it, I said I did not want to live in Canada. I told him once my assignment was over, I wanted to go back home to my family and friends. He said okay. My assignment was finally up. Alan and I flew back together. I know he was ready to go because he made business calls and made business deals almost all day. He needed to be in his office. We arrived back safely. Alan appeared to be so happy.

Darlene was in town also. I met her at five o'clock. She said that she had ordered our favorite meal and was ready to talk about everything. In a matter of twenty minutes, I had told her everything. She looked at me, and for ten minutes, she did not say anything. She asked lots of questions, but the one that I could not answer was if I were pregnant, who was the father. My eyes got bigger, and I got an instant headache. I started scratching my head and began stuttering. She looked at me and said, "You did not think about that?" She began to tell me about some awkward situations I would find myself in if Josh was the father of the child. I told her to quit asking questions. I told her that I was not pregnant. I told her that nothing happened with Josh. I told her that I felt bad enough and that I did not want to think about that anymore. She said maybe this time she would be a godmother. She said, "Maybe you will have twins. One will be Josh, and one will be Alan." I just looked at Darlene. I knew she did not believe me. I could hear some anger in her voice. Darlene and I were like sisters;

Alan was like her brother-in-law. He had acted stupid, but Darlene was able to forgive him. She asked me if I was going to tell Alan. She said that Alan had not been in my life for quite a while, and things happen. I told her that I had not thought about telling anyone but her. She said she thought I should consider being honest. I told her that I was sorry about the way I had behaved. She told me to tell Alan that also. She asked me if I had realized that I had committed adultery and if I realized what God was thinking about as it related to Josh and me. I had nothing to say. She said she would be with me, but this was a situation that I needed to seek God for answers. She told me I needed to repent. I told her that I was sorry that I allowed Josh to spend that time with me.

Since moving to Canada, Darlene and Troy had been going to a church not far from their house. They had invited me several times, but I did not go. They stayed in church almost every week. Darlene's life had changed. She was talking more about God and how much He loved us. She told me that they had joined the church and that she and Troy were born again believers. I did not ask too many questions. She talked more about God than anything. She was still there for me, but most of the time, she told me about getting my life right with God.

Darlene talked about her mom and things that were going on with their life. Her daughter, my goddaughter, was growing up. She showed me pictures of her cheering. I apologized for not going to one of her games while I was in Canada. I promised her that the next time we came, either Alan or I would attend.

Darlene hugged me and told me she had to meet Troy. She told me to call her later.

Three months passed before I went to the doctor. I was feeling nauseous almost every morning. Alan and I were doing fine. We had reunited, and life was great. Alan was in Canada a lot doing business. He had looked at several houses and talked about moving there. He felt Canada would be a place where we could make a clean start. He felt good about it because Darlene and Troy were there. He really wanted to move. He had told me several times how my job could transfer me there.

Josh had not called. I assumed he knew that Alan and I had gotten our life together, and we were moving in the right direction. I had not told Alan about the appointment, I was just going. I did not want Alan to get excited. I felt this time I would handle everything differently.

The doctor came out smiling. He said that in a matter of months, I would be a proud mother. He asked me who the father was. I told him, and he said great. He could not wait to meet him.

I left the doctor's office happy. I could not wait to tell Alan. The telephone rang, and it was Josh. Since he was on the phone, I decided to tell him the good news. I told him that I was pregnant. He said great. He could not wait to be a father. I told him that Alan was the father, and he asked me if I was sure. I dropped the phone. All of a sudden, I realized that Josh could be the father also. I told Josh that I would call him back. I called Darlene and told her that I needed to meet her.

She met me in the cafeteria in the hospital. She asked me if I was pregnant. I told her that I was. She said that she hoped everything would go fine this time. She said that she and Troy would start praying for me to have a healthy baby. She was going on and on. She even asked me if I was going to name the baby after Alan. I looked at her and told her that I did not know who the father was. She stopped, looked at me, and said Alan has to be the father. I reminded her of the last conversation we had about an awkward situation. I told her that this was the situation that she was talking about. She said she just believed that Alan's baby was growing inside of me. She said she had to go. She invited us to her church. She said it would start at seven. She gave me the address and ran off.

Darlene was talking to Alan when I walked out of the door. Alan said that he was on his way to get a bite to eat. He said he talked to Troy earlier and they were going bowling that night. He asked me if I had plans with Darlene. I told him that I had not made a decision about church, but I would let him know. I kissed Alan on his cheek and told him that I would see him later. After Alan walked away, I told Darlene that I would give him the news later.

I went to church with Darlene. I had not been to church for a long time. The choir and the sermon were great. It seemed as if the pastor was talking to me. All of a sudden, tears starting flowing and flowing. I could not stop. Darlene looked at me and told me that everything would be okay. The pastor asked if there was anyone that needed prayer or wanted to give their life to the Lord. I had heard this statement so much. I just wiped my tears and looked around to see who was getting up. Before I knew anything, I was going up to the altar. Darlene was right behind me. I accepted God in my life and became a born-again believer. I was so happy. Darlene just hugged me. She told me God had forgiven me, and He would work everything out for me. She introduced me to the pastor, his wife, and other people in the church. I did not realize how many people Darlene knew. She had been there for a while. She also told me about some classes that she suggested I take. I told her that I would probably sign up for some of them later. She told me to stay with God, read my Bible, believe, and trust Him, no matter what happens. I told her I would.

Driving back home was hard. I knew I had to be honest with Alan. When I got home, Alan had prepared a late-night snack. He told me that he was waiting up for me. I told him what happened at church. He said he was happy for me. He told me about bowling and how he and Troy had a great time. He told me to sit with him for a while. He told me how much he loved me and how much he wanted to be near me. He told me that no matter how angry he got that he would never leave me again. I told him that I wanted to talk to him about what God had done in my life and other things. He said it could wait. He said all he wanted to do was spend time with his wife. He picked me up and took me to the bedroom. Alan was so romantic. As I laid in bed, watching him as he slept, I knew that his joy and laughter would turn to frowns, sadness, and tears.

I got out of bed, went into the living room, and began reading the Bible. I turned to the story of David and Bathsheba (2 Samuel 11). Tears rolled down my cheeks as I wondered what I had done to my marriage. All of a sudden, I heard a noise. I looked back and saw Alan standing near me. He sat down and took my hand and asked me what was wrong. He kissed me on the cheek and told me to tell him what was bothering me. He told me that he had been married to his best friend and best friends talk to each other. He said that he and Troy had a conversation about God and how God wanted the best for him and his life. He said that Troy had a very interesting conversation. He said that he told Troy he was going to talk to me about us visiting the church and developing a closer relationship with God. He said that he wanted God to be a part of our marriage and our life. I told him that I had given my life to God at church. I told him that I accepted God in my life, and I repeated Romans 10:9. He asked what that was. I showed it to him in the Bible. He grabbed my hand, and we repeated the verse together. We embraced and started talking about attending the church on Sunday. He kissed me and said he wanted to learn more about God and how He could change our lives. He said that he knew that God must love him because He put me in his life. He asked me to forgive him for everything he had done. He said that he was mean to me and he hurt me. He said that he wanted me to know that would never happen again.

I looked at him and began to cry. He asked me what was wrong. I looked at him and told him that I was pregnant. Alan picked me up, kissed me, and said God was answering prayers already. He said that if he had known that was all he had to say to see such a quick reply, he would have recited Romans 10:9 years ago. He looked at me and said this time, nothing will go wrong. I looked at him and cried more and more. He looked puzzled and asked why I was not happy. I told him that I had done a terrible thing. I told him that I had something to share, and I should have shared years ago. He told me to take my time and tell him. He said that he wanted this to be a new beginning for both of us. I told him that depending on how he felt about me after I gave him the news, that this day could possibly end our marriage. I told him that if it did, I would understand, and I would just have to depend on God to help me. He told me to tell him what was on my mind.

I told him everything. I told him how I met Josh, how I spent time with him, and when I met his family. I told him about the telephone calls, letters, and cards. I told him about our last time together. I told him I loved him. Alan looked at me. Tears rolled down his face. He walked out of the room. He walked back in and asked me about the child. I told him that I was not sure. I told him I could be carrying another man's child. His whole body shook. He grabbed me and held me so tight. He continued to squeeze me. I was sure I had marks on my arms. He shook me and asked me how I let this happen. He asked me who and what did he marry. He told me that he had been living a lie for years. I tried to explain. I tried to tell him what happened. He grabbed his coat and walked out. I went into the bedroom, threw myself on the bed, and cried and cried.

Hour passed. I felt miserable. All of a sudden, the telephone rang. I did not know whether to pick it up or not. I could not talk to Josh. The two of us had done enough. We did not need to talk to each other. The telephone continued to ring; I picked it up, and it was Darlene. She asked me if I was okay. I told her no. She told me that Alan was on his way home. She said that he had been with them since midnight. She said she was sure Alan was feeling better. She said Troy wanted me to call you and let you know that everything would work out for the best. I thanked her and told her that I would wait for Alan.

Alan arrived almost an hour later. He walked in, kissed me on my forehead, and said that he had to digest the information. He said it would take him some time, but he was going to try to work through the information. He said that Troy and Darlene prayed with him. He told me that he was not sure how he felt. He asked me if I had talked to Josh. I told him I did, but I also told him that I would end everything with Josh. He looked at me and said it should never have started. Alan was angry. He was trying to be calm, but every now and then, he would raise his voice. I told Alan I really wanted him to be the father. He asked me if I was sure he was the father. I told him that I was not sure, but we would find out. He said that he guessed all he could do was hope. He stormed out of the room and went into the bedroom. He slammed the door. I waited patiently to see what he would do. He came out and said that he was moving to the basement for a while. He said that he needed time to think. I told him that I understood. He said he was hoping and praying that this was his child and he was hoping that everything would go okay. He said that he promised God, Darlene, and Troy that he would stay and make some serious decisions after the baby was born. He also told me to please end the relationship I had with Josh because he could not be responsible for his actions if Josh came to his house or if Josh was the father of the baby. I promised him I would. He said that he would support me and be there for me. He said he was not going to leave the baby and me.

Alan and I lived separately in the house. We talked every day. He was there for all of my appointments. When the doctor would say you must be a proud father, Alan would look at me. I guess I could not ask for anything else. We would go to dinner and sometimes to a movie. He really did have a different attitude than before. We would go to church together. His mom came to visit us a couple of times. She was very lonesome since her husband's death. We promised her that we would always be there for her.

She saw our living arrangement and asked Alan why he was sleeping in the basement. He told her that he wanted to give me some space. She accepted what he said and did not ask any more questions. Everyone felt good about this pregnancy. I had made eight months. I could barely work, and Alan was there to help me every step of the way. Whatever I wanted, he would get it for me. We talked more and laughed more. It seemed as if Alan was really feeling differently about me. He would talk about how he was going to spend time with his child and all the things he wanted to do with him. He was so sure it was going to be a boy. I decided that we would just wait until the child was born to see the sex of the child. I tried to avoid all kinds of test. I would find out the father of the child soon enough.

I felt so heavy. I got up to go to the kitchen, and then it happened. I had read enough books and had talked to Darlene about this. I called her because Alan was out of town on business and was supposed to arrive home that afternoon. Darlene and Troy came. They got me to the hospital in town. I could not believe I was having a baby. This was the first time I had actually made it to the delivery room. Alan arrived right on time. He said he took an early flight because he felt the baby was going to come. We were so happy. He was right there for me. He told me that he loved me.

I had an eight-pound baby boy. Alan said he wanted to name him Darren after my biological father. He kissed me on my cheek and smiled. He told me how happy he was, and he was going to enjoy being a father. I looked at him wondering if he knew something I did not know. By this time the doctor came in. He said he wanted to talk to both of us. Alan was so happy, he just started thanking him for all that he had done. Dr. Morris looked at him and said, "We need to talk." He told us that Darren had some problems breathing. He said he had respiratory problems and his heart was too large. We both looked at him. He said that there was a problem with his kidney also. He said that he was sure Darren would not make it. Alan fell on the floor. I just looked shocked. Alan asked the doctor if God was punishing us. The doctor told him that he did not think it was anyone's fault. Tears rolled down my eyes. I could not believe any of this. I had a baby boy for one hour and now he was dying. Darlene and Troy walked in. We told them the news. All of us cried. Ten hours later, we had a memorial service for him at the hospital. I had lost another child.

Two weeks passed. The telephone rang. I thought it was Alan, but it was Josh. I told him what had happened, and I told him it was over. He said that he was sorry. He said that he understood and that he was moving home with his parents because his father was very sick. He said that he wanted me to be happy. I told him I was happy with my husband. He told me goodbye, and I put the telephone down. I sat quietly for minutes, but I knew this was how it had to end. I told Alan about the conversation. He thanked me for ending the relationship. He moved back into the bedroom.

Years passed, and Alan and I were so happy. So much had gone on in our lives. We lost babies; Alan's father died. My stepfather was in a rehabilitation center. He had fallen and broken his hip. My mom was doing okay, but we would make trips often to check on all of them. Alan's Mom was okay. She seemed to be adjusting more and more; but she missed her husband. Darlene and Troy were ordained ministers in their church. We were members of the same church. I was teaching

Sunday school. Alan was just going on business trips, getting promotions on his job, and enjoying life. Everything was going great until I started feeling sick. I was feeling awful. I had been sick for about two weeks. I just could not shake this bad feeling. I talked to Alan. He had tried all of our home remedies. Nothing worked. I talked to Darlene. We prayed, but I seemed to have been getting worse. I made an appointment and Darlene went with me. I was a little frightened because I did not know what the doctor was going to find. Alan was at work, and whatever the doctor said, I wanted to tell him myself.

I had done so many tests. I sat with Darlene, waiting for the results. I prayed silently to myself that whatever it was, God would instantly heal me. I did not want to think of the worst, so I tried to stay focus on positive things. Life was so good for us; there was no time for me to get sick. Darlene must have been feeling the same way because she was so quiet. Darlene talked all the time.

The doctor came out and told me that he had some good news and some bad news. Darlene and I stood up at the same time. He said that he would start with the good news. I was three months. I asked the doctor what he meant. Darlene was jumping up and down. He said that there was a baby inside of me. I almost fainted. Alan and I had really not talked about a baby since Darren. We both avoided the discussion. The doctor said that the bad news was that probably around the sixth or seventh month, I would need to be on bed rest because of what my body had been through. I asked the doctor if I had any other sickness. He said no. I was fine.

Alan sat very quietly when I told him the news. He walked into the kitchen and started to prepare dinner. I asked him if he heard what I said. He said yes, but he did not want to get too excited. He said he did not want to tell anyone but Darlene and Troy. He said he could not face any more disappointments. He said more than ever, he was concerned about my health. He said that I was older and he did not want anything to happen to me. I told him that God was not going to let us down. I told him that God loved us. He wanted us to have a baby, and this would be the time. Alan looked at me and said that he was hoping I was right. He said that as always, he would not let me go through this alone.

Age probably had a lot to do with my pregnancy. I was not real sick, but I stayed tired a lot. I was glad when the doctor put me on bed rest. Everyone was so good to me. My job was very supportive. We did tell some more of our friends. I am glad we did because they would come around when Alan was on business trips to take care of me. Darlene and Troy would spend the night sometimes. We told our parents. My stepfather was so excited. His prayer was that God would allow him to see his grandchild. He was better and he had moved back home with my mother. The neighbors were helpful. They were looking out for both of them. We were not able to go home as often because the long ride was not good for me.

It was déjà vu. I got up to go to the bathroom and it happened. Water was everywhere. I called Darlene. Alan was on his way home. He had taken an earlier flight because of my due date. Darlene got me to the hospital just in time. Alan made it in the delivery room. All I could do was think about Darren and pray. Alan grabbed my hand and said we are going to have a child this time. I could barely answer; I was hurting so badly. Dr. Morris continued to say push. Alan was wiping my brow and getting on my nerves. I could not wait for this to be over. Dr. Morris was talking about something. It seemed as if I was in and out of consciousness. I heard Dr. Morris say, "Oh my goodness." In all my pain, it seemed as if my heart fainted. All I could think about was that it was happening again. He said with a much louder voice, "Oh my goodness! There is another one." I heard something hit the floor. The nurse said Alan had fainted. One of the nurses ran to help him. I was still trying to figure out what was going on. I heard crying and then Dr. Morris say, "He is going to be okay; he is the proud father of twins." I was speechless.

Nicholas and Nicholett were the cutest babies I had ever seen. We had two six-pound babies—a boy and a girl. God gave us the desires of our heart. Alan was a proud father, and I was a happy mother. It was only God who could answer our prayers and give us this great gift. These babies grew and grew and grew.

All Alone

In the corner of the room, I sat all alone. The only noise I heard was the roar of the heater, and I saw a glimmer of light peeping through the window that seemed to smile at me. The room was decorated beautifully. The colors on the wall seemed to envelop me with warmth and love. On my left were abstract paintings that seemed to tell the story of successes and failures in life. On my right were paintings of great African American heroes. In front of me was a big map of Africa with rivers that seemed to flow forever. Behind me were two enormous windows dressed with long blue satin curtains with navy blue sashes on each side that reminded me of an endless dance.

In this room, I sat all alone not knowing if I would ever leave or if anyone would ever find me. In this room, I heard a thunderous voice say, "Come unto Me and I give you the rest and the peace that you have been searching for forever and forever; I will allow you to enter the gateways of freedom."

In this room, I sat all alone, knowing that I was locked behind a bolted door that would never open. I knew I was shut off from the world. I was in the dark and even light would refuse to enter. I wondered about the voice. Who would be concerned about me? Who could this be? What had I done to deserve someone even thinking about me? Who would be willing to be condemned with me? I wondered if I would hear this voice again. I wondered if I would answer. I wondered if this was just my imagination playing tricks on me.

In this room, I sat all alone, knowing that He had the key and that He was the only one that could open the gateway of the unforeseen present and an outstanding future. Then, I felt His presence. It was as though His whole body consumed mine. It was as if we became one. I listened intently. I sat quietly. I tried not to move. I tried not to make a sound.

In the corner of the room, I sat all alone. There He reached out for me. I sat quietly, I listened, and then I reached out to Him. He took my hand; I got up and followed Jesus and life began anew.

Also available from the author:

Creations from the Heart
ISBN 9780615525679

Available at Amazon, Barnes and Noble,
or wherever books are sold

Contact Information

The author is available for book signings, book readings, and other speaking opportunities.

You may contact her by writing to:

Mable I. Cox
P. O. Box 441035
Fort Washington, MD 20744